Also by Jan

Detective Parker Bell Series

A SECRET TO THE GRAVE
WINTER WONDERLAND
DEAD OR ALIVE
LITTLE GIRL LOST
FORGOTTEN

Count to Ten Series

ONE
TWO
THREE
FOUR
FIVE
SIX
BURNING SECRETS
SEVEN
EIGHT
NINE
TEN

Broken Gems Series

CRACKED SAPPHIRE
CRUSHED RUBY
FRACTURED DIAMOND
SHATTERED AMETHYST
SPLINTERED EMERALD
SALVAGING MARIGOLD

River's End Rescues Series

COCKY SAVIOR
SOME REGRETS ARE FOREVER
PROTECT
SOME LIES WILL HAUNT YOU

SOME QUESTIONS HAVE NO ANSWERS
SOME TRUTH CAN BE DISTORTED
SOME TRUST CAN BE REBUILT
SOME MISTAKES ARE UNFORGIVABLE

Saving SEALs Series

SAVING RYDER
SAVING ERIC
SAVING OWEN
SAVING LOGAN
SAVING GRAYSON
SAVING CHARLIE

Christmas Romantic Suspense Series

CHRISTMAS HOSTAGE
CHRISTMAS CAPTIVE
CHRISTMAS VICTIM
YULETIDE PROTECTOR

Some Mistakes Are Unforgivable

Jane Blythe

Bear Spots Publications
Melbourne Australia

Paperback
ISBN-13: 978-0-6452796-4-1

Cover designed by QDesigns

I'd like to thank everyone who played a part in bringing this story to life. Particularly my mom who is always there to share her thoughts and opinions with me. My awesome cover designer, Amy, who whips up covers for me so quickly and who patiently makes every change I ask for, and there are usually lots of them! And my lovely editor Lisa Edwards, for all their encouragement and for all the hard work they put into polishing my work.

MARCH 20TH

8:59 P.M.

She had made a horrific mistake.

A mistake she couldn't ever take back.

Fifteen-year-old Dahlia Black wished with all her heart that she had listened to her parents.

Instead, she had defied them and been lured into a trap.

A trap she should have seen.

But no, she'd been so stupidly naïve. She had thought it was just her parents being ridiculously overprotective. With three older brothers and two older cousins who were like big brothers in the military, Dahlia was used to stifling protectiveness.

She'd just wanted to do her own thing.

Build her own life.

Make her own choices.

Instead, she and her two best friends were locked in cages like animals. A screen hung on the wall on the other side of the warehouse with three columns on it. One had an R at the top, another a T, and the third a K. Underneath each letter were three ever-changing numbers.

Unfortunately, she knew what the letters and numbers meant.

Her abductors hadn't been shy in telling them exactly what was going to happen to them. They were part of some dark web game where men with more money than morals paid to vote on which of her friends would receive which punishment.

An alarm sounded, and she shrunk further back against the

metal bars. She didn't want to be here, she wanted to be back home. She would gladly take her parents and brothers over-protectiveness for the rest of her life if they would just come running through the door right now.

"Voting for game twenty-two has now closed, and we have our winners," a man announced to a camera. He was dressed in a tuxedo with a white mask that covered his entire face. A bright red mouth and black circles around the eyes gave it a creepy look. "Our pretty brunette will be killed, the blonde won for being tortured, and the sweet little redhead will be raped. I think I hit the jackpot on that one."

No.

This couldn't be happening.

It couldn't be real.

And yet a second later a gunshot rang out and her best friend since they were two, Alicia Colton, dropped to the floor in her cell beside Dahlia's, a hole in her forehead, her dark eyes staring sightlessly across the space between them.

Accusingly.

This was all her fault.

She was the one who had decided that she wanted to be a model and had taken the card the supposed modeling agent had given her when she and her friends had been out riding their horses. She was the one who had defied her parents when they told her she couldn't go to an interview with the agency but had convinced her friends to skip school with her to go anyway.

Alicia's death was her fault.

Someone was screaming.

Brynn.

Her other best friend was in the cage on Dahlia's left, her blue eyes locked on Alicia's lifeless body, sobbing and screaming hysterically.

Dahlia wanted to say something to comfort Brynn, but what was there to say?

The voters had chosen Alicia to die, Brynn to be tortured, and her to be raped.

She had never thought she would have to say that word in the same sentence as her name.

They were trapped. They'd been drugged at the interview and woken up naked here in these cells who knows how many days ago. They'd been kept here, given scraps of food and the occasional bottle of water, while the game played out and the votes came in. There was no hope, when the game was over she and Brynn would be killed or sold, they would never be heard from again, and she doubted her family would ever know what happened to her.

Her cell door was unlocked, the man in the tuxedo and scary mask stepped inside. As he walked toward her, Dahlia scampered away from him, desperate to stop the inevitable from happening even as she knew there was no escape. There were a dozen men here, all of them dressed in suits and the same creepy mask as the man advancing on her, all of them armed. Even if she made it out of her cage she wasn't escaping the warehouse, she wasn't finding salvation.

Her fate had been sealed the moment she made the decision to defy her parents.

The man reached her and backhanded her hard enough that she saw stars. By the time the pain cleared enough that she could think, he was already violating her.

Tears streamed down her face, she tried to block out what was happening, but the only other thing to focus on was Brynn's screams as two men tied her to a chair. Both of the men were dressed in what she thought looked like those suits that crime scene people wore so they didn't contaminate crime scenes.

Dahlia felt her stomach drop as she realized what that meant.

They didn't want Brynn's blood on them when they tortured her.

Her friend's screams of agony burrowed deep into her soul.

It was her fault Alicia was dead.

It was her fault Brynn was being hurt.

All her fault.

She wished she had been the one who had been killed.

The air suddenly filled with the sound of gunfire.

What was going on?

To be honest, at this point Dahlia didn't really care. When the tuxedo man climbed off her, she simply curled herself into a small ball, tucked her knees to her chest, buried her face in her hands, and sobbed.

How could one mistake cause this much destruction?

She hadn't meant for any of this to happen. She'd just wanted a way to get out of her small town, out from under the strict rules her parents enforced, out from under the pressures of having basically five over-protective big brothers.

She'd just wanted to find herself.

In the end, what she had found out about herself she didn't like at all. She was a selfish, spoiled brat who had gotten her friends abducted, hurt, and killed.

Hands closed around her shoulders, but she ignored them, she didn't want to look up, didn't want to see the tuxedo man or any of the others.

"Dahlia."

Startled at hearing the familiar masculine voice say her name, she lifted her tear-streaked face to see a man dressed in tactical gear on his knees beside her.

She knew that face.

Those eyes.

It was her brother Theo's best friend, Fletcher. She'd had a crush on him since she was ten, but he just saw her as Theo's baby sister.

What was he doing here?

"It's okay, sweetheart," he murmured, "you're safe now. We'll get you out of here."

We?

Were her brothers here too?

As much as she longed to see them, longed to know that she and Brynn—if her friend was still alive—were safe, she was so ashamed for anyone to see her.

Fletcher stripped off his Kevlar vest and pulled his t-shirt over his head, slipping it on her, dressing her as though she were a child.

"There you go, honey," he said, cupping one of her cheeks in his large hand, his thumb brushing lightly across the skin just under where her face throbbed from tuxedo man's blow.

His blue eyes were kind, his smile reassuring, his touch comforting, and she thought that maybe everything could somehow be okay.

But then he grunted, his eyes widening as blood bloomed on his chest.

He'd been shot.

Because he'd taken his bullet proof vest off to give her his t-shirt so she wouldn't be naked.

Dahlia lost it. She sobbed and screamed as Fletcher's large body slumped against her, pinning her against the metal bars. He was dead because of her, this was all her fault. How would she face Theo after getting his best friend killed? How would she face Brynn if her friend was still alive? How would she face Alicia's family? How would she face her own?

How would she face herself?

The weight of Fletcher's body was pulled off her and then a hand smoothed her hair. "It's okay, Dahlia, Fletcher isn't dead. Just hold on, sweetie, and we'll get you out of here," Theo said as he continued to stroke her hair in an effort to soothe her.

"I'm okay, Dahlia," Fletcher grunted, voice tight with pain.

No.

He wasn't.

He'd been shot.

Nothing about this was okay.

"Theo, is she all right?" Levi asked, appearing beside them as he knelt next to Fletcher.

Theo's hand moved to her neck to check her pulse. "I see blood on her face, and …" he swore, "and blood between her legs."

Levi swore too. "Let's get her out of here and then I'll check her out."

Shame burned hot inside her, and then as Theo gently scooped her into his arms, icy cold shock took over. She trembled violently. Tears streamed down her face, she had a headache and an ache between her legs that reminded her of what she had lost in this warehouse.

Theo carried her away, and she was aware of Levi helping Fletcher walk beside them. The shooting had stopped, and she saw bodies everywhere she looked.

So much death.

So much pain.

So much suffering.

Everything hit her like a ton of bricks, the realization that she would never be the same, her life would never be the same, overwhelmed, Dahlia didn't fight it when the world spiraled around her and black dots danced in front of her eyes, she let shock pull her under and fainted dead away.

THREE YEARS LATER
JUNE 26TH

9:00 A.M.

It was finally here.

The day she had been counting down to for three years, three months, and six days had finally arrived, and for the first time in all those years, Dahlia felt like she could breathe again.

She was free.

Looking back, Dahlia wasn't even sure how she had made it through the aftermath of her ordeal. She'd been carried out of the warehouse in her brother Theo's arms, examined by her doctor brother Levi because he was the only medical professional there that she would allow to touch her, and then came the questions.

So many questions.

While no one outright said the words, she could feel the recrimination in each law enforcement officer who spoke to her. A silent question hung between them. How could she have been so stupid?

Three years later, Dahlia still didn't have an answer to that.

But now she was free, she could finally leave River's End, and she wasn't ever coming back here. Not for anything.

Not even her family.

They hadn't abandoned her even with the unforgivable mistake she'd made, but she felt their disappointment in her every time she saw them, and the weight of it was crushing her.

She had to leave.

For her sanity it was the only option.

With a last look around her bedroom, Dahlia picked up the suitcase that contained all she intended to take with her and walked out into the hall. It felt sad closing the door behind her, that room had been her little sanctuary from her full-on family over the years. It had been her safe haven these last three years, the only place she could relax away from prying eyes.

Now it was time to say goodbye.

To her room, to her home, to her family, to the town she had lived in all her life, and after the mess her life had become, Dahlia wasn't surprised that much stronger than the wisp of sadness she felt was the relief.

Trudging down the stairs, both her parents looked up when she walked into the kitchen, suitcase in tow.

Her mom jumped up from her chair at the table. "Dahlia?"

"I'm leaving," she said simply. She had prepared herself to have this conversation ever since she had come up with this plan. She had the next stage of her life all mapped out. She would be moving to San Diego, with two jobs lined up to pay her way through college—no way did she feel she deserved to have her parents' hard earned money pay her way after she had defied them and ruined her own life and her friends'—one of which would be cleaning offices at a rehab center that worked mainly with military men and women injured in combat. Her end goal was to become a physical therapist and maybe undo a little of the bad she had caused by helping those who were brave, strong and dedicated their lives to making the world a better place.

"You only graduated yesterday," her father said.

Dahlia nodded. What was there to say? She knew yesterday had been her high school graduation, she'd been counting down to it for the past three years.

The back door opened and her oldest brother Abe walked through it. He caught sight of the suitcase, looked from her to their parents and back again. "You going somewhere, kiddo?" he asked in his gruff way.

"Yes, San Diego," she replied.

Her mom gasped. "That's so far. Couldn't you have gone to college somewhere closer? Somewhere where you could have continued to live at home with us?"

Of course she *could* have.

But she didn't *want* to.

She wanted to get as far away from here as she could so she was literally fleeing to the other side of the country.

The truth of the matter was, she just couldn't spend another day here in this house, crushed by the weight of her mistakes. Still, she could see why this would be surprising to her parents, she hadn't stepped foot off their land since she was brought back here after her brothers and the FBI rescued her. She couldn't face the looks of blame she was sure she would see on the town's residents, so she had refused to leave and no one had ever tried to make her.

Because they knew.

They knew what the town's residents would say to her, and they agreed.

So, they had let her hide out here, finishing high school online, no proms or homecoming for her, not that she'd wanted them anyway.

All she wanted was to do the best she could to make up for her mistake that had gotten Alicia killed, Brynn maimed, and herself sexually assaulted.

"I don't want to stay here, Mom," she said simply. Her mom flinched, but Dahlia just shrugged, it was what it was, and truth be told, she was sure that once the shock wore off her parents would be glad to see her gone.

"You don't need to run away, sweetheart," her mom said, cautiously closing the space between them but not touching her. Her family had quickly learned that she did not like to be touched.

By anyone.

Not even her family.

Being touched always gave her a flashback to her assault and as was her pattern she avoided anything and everything that caused her pain.

"I'm going, Mom. I'm going to UCSD, I have two jobs lined up to pay for it, and I've already rented an apartment. I'm leaving, and I won't be coming back. Ever," she added just to be clear.

Her mom's face crumpled, but Dahlia refused to get sucked into staying here. She just couldn't. She wasn't trying to hurt her family—goodness knows she'd done enough of that to last a lifetime—it was just that she absolutely could not remain here. If she did, she was terrified she would slowly waste away until her only option left was to take her own life.

She'd thought about it a lot, especially in the early days after her assault, but in the end, she could never go through with it because if she did, she could never make up for the mistakes she'd made and the damage she'd caused. The only way to do that was to live, to help others.

"Sweetheart, I wish you could forgive yourself." Mom grabbed her and dragged her into a tight hug, one Dahlia struggled to return. "You made one little youthful mistake, baby. What happened wasn't your fault. Can't you find a way to forgive yourself?"

The answer to that was simple.

No.

She couldn't.

She didn't bother saying it because all four people in the room already knew that she wouldn't ever forgive herself for what she'd done.

Carefully, she stepped out of her mother's embrace and looked at the clock on the wall. "I have to go, my flight is at twelve."

Tears in her eyes, her mom nodded. "Dad and I will drive you to the airport."

"That's not necessary, I'm taking a cab," she said.

"Dahlia," her mom looked aghast.

"I'm taking a cab," she said firmly.

"Like Hell you are," Abe said. "If you don't want Mom and Dad to take you then I'll drive you."

Between the two that was the better option and she knew better than to argue with her oldest brother. Abe was gruff, quiet, borderline intimidating, and she was the least close to him of her three big brothers simply because of the ten-year age difference.

"I can't believe you're leaving," Mom said, crying in earnest now.

"I have to," she said.

"I wish you could forgive yourself." After a brief hesitation, Mom hugged her again, then her dad stepped up.

"We are always here for you, princess, you need anything you call," he told her. Dahlia nodded but knew she would never reach out to them for help, they had already done more for her than she deserved. When her dad pulled her into his arms her heart almost cracked in two, she knew that she was making the right decision for all of them, but it didn't mean she wasn't going to miss them.

"Bye," she said softly, as Abe took her suitcase and she followed him out to his truck.

As they drove away, the last thing she saw was her parents standing at the front door, holding onto each other and crying. Dahlia closed her eyes, fighting back tears of her own, and rested her head against the window.

They didn't talk during the long drive to the airport, didn't talk as Abe parked and got her suitcase out. Dahlia had turned and started walking away before her big brother finally said something.

"Dahlia, we love you, all of us, no one ever blamed you for what happened, and if you don't learn how to forgive yourself, you're never going to find peace."

She didn't deserve peace.

People had died because of her mistake.

"Cut yourself a break. You were only fifteen, and those men knew what they were doing. They played you, it's not your fault that you fell for it. Please, try to believe that, we all hate seeing you hurting like this and not be able to make it better."

Which was one of the reasons she was leaving. She couldn't make her family live through her mistakes any longer.

"We love you, kid, always and unconditionally. When you're ready to come home you know we'll all be here waiting for you."

Dahlia nodded then turned to leave, knowing this was it, she was never coming back.

She got only a few steps before a large hand covered her shoulder.

"I know you hate being touched, but I can't let my baby sister leave without holding her one last time." With surprising gentleness, the large man pulled her into his arms.

It was Abe's hug that nearly broke her.

Her family was all so strong, so tough, so brave, and honorable too. They'd all served in the military, Levi was still active service, they were everything she wished she could be but knew she couldn't.

Abe released her after a long minute, bent to kiss her forehead, then straightened and walked back to his car.

Dahlia watched him drive away, her heart in a million pieces. Her life was a mess, she'd hurt her family, and now she had to move forward alone.

Leaving was definitely harder than she had thought it would be when she walked out of her bedroom this morning, but it was the only way.

Fighting back tears, Dahlia turned and headed into the airport.

FIVE YEARS LATER
JUNE 11TH

10:15 P.M.

It was definitely a mistake to be back here.

Dahlia had vowed she would never set foot in this town again and yet here she was. Almost five years to the day that she had left, and now she was driving through the streets she used to know so well.

She didn't want to be here, absolutely not her choice, but her mother had begged and pleaded, and in the end, Dahlia had caved and agreed to get on a flight and come to River's End. She had however refused to allow anyone to pick her up from the airport, knowing that this wasn't going to be easy and that she would need the time alone to get herself together before she drove her rental car into town.

And now here she was, driving through River's End on her way to the hospital.

It felt weird being back here.

And not good weird.

The kind of horrible weird that filled you with tension, a snake of dread coiled in her gut, ready to strike her with overwhelming panic at a moment's notice.

She shouldn't have come.

She'd known it and should never have allowed herself to be talked into it.

It wasn't that she wasn't excited and thrilled for her big brother Abe and the new little addition to his family, it was just that she would have preferred to wait until he, his new wife Meadow, and their newborn daughter Dawn could get on a plane and visit her in San Diego.

Her family's lives were changing, and for the first time in the five years since she had left, she felt like she was missing out by not having them close by. At first she had loved the freedom afforded by living on the opposite side of the country, the noose of guilt around her neck began to loosen, and she loved her studies and her work at the rehab facility. But then Abe had met and married Meadow, and Theo was engaged to and expecting a baby with long-term family friend Maggie Wilson, and according to a recent text from her mom, even Levi was interested in the new deputy Sydney Clark.

They were all moving on with their lives, finding happiness, starting families of their own, while she went home to her apartment alone every night.

She could admit she was lonely; she just wasn't going to do anything about it.

She couldn't.

She was responsible for the deaths of her two best friends. Alicia had died that day in the warehouse, just minutes before they were rescued, and Brynn had committed suicide almost three years ago, unable to deal with the ongoing trauma of their ordeal.

Most days Dahlia had no idea how she managed to deal with it either.

There wasn't time to dwell on it—probably how she survived, keeping herself too busy to think—because she had reached the hospital. She parked her car in the underground garage of the hospital that serviced River's End and the neighboring towns and climbed out.

Her knees were shaking so badly she had to lock them together to keep from sinking to the hard concrete ground and giving in to the panic swirling inside her. This was a quick in and out visit, she already had a flight booked for six in the morning, and she would leave as soon as she had met her new baby niece, but she would be here long enough that someone could see her.

Dahlia locked her rental car and walked toward the elevator because she had committed to this and didn't have a choice. All she could do was hope that her disguise—yes, she was lame enough to come wearing one because she didn't want anyone in town to come and speak to her—was enough to hide her identity. No one in town had seen her in over eight years, so she hoped the wide-brimmed white straw hat and sunglasses would hide her very noticeable red hair and most of her face.

Fingers crossed.

Dahlia was about halfway across the parking garage when she became aware of another presence. You didn't suffer PTSD and become hyperaware of your surroundings and not notice when anyone was approaching your personal space.

Fear swept through her, she hated it, hated that because of one stupid teenage mistake her whole life revolved around fear, and when she realized that whoever it was was gaining on her, she reached into her purse for her mace and spun around ready to spray it if she needed it.

A huge man was just a few steps behind her, and she couldn't stop a scream from falling from her lips as she sprayed the mace.

The man sidestepped the spray and grabbed hold of her, pinning her against a rock-hard chest, her arms trapped at her sides, a large hand covering her mouth, leaving her virtually defenseless.

No.

She would never be helpless again.

Ever.

If he thought he could just grab her and drag her away then he was sorely mistaken.

Dahlia began to fight with everything she had, kicking her legs and clawing with her fingers as she tried to bite the hand preventing her from screaming for help.

It wasn't until she heard the soft voice murmuring in her ear that she realized she'd made a mistake.

All at once she stopped fighting.

"Shh, sweetheart, it's Fletcher, you're okay," the voice whispered. When he seemed confident that she had heard him he slowly released her and Dahlia dragged in several deep breaths in what felt like a futile attempt to still her racing heart.

"I didn't realize it was you," she said, embarrassed now that she knew she wasn't about to be raped or murdered.

"It's fine, honey," he assured her. "I'm sorry, I didn't mean to scare you. I just saw you get out of the car and came up to say hi. Didn't realize you were going to going to go all warrior princess on me. I hope I didn't hurt you, just didn't want to get an eyeful of that stuff, it's the worst to clean out." Even though she couldn't see him she could tell he was smiling, trying to tease her, help her calm down.

"It's okay," she said softly. She hadn't moved away from Fletcher. Her back was still pressed up against his front, and while he wasn't holding her tightly, his arm still banded across her waist. Usually, she hated for anyone to touch her, but Fletcher's hold didn't ignite a fire of panic inside her.

Actually it did the opposite.

Desire curled inside her, catching her unawares. She may have had a crush on Fletcher since she first started noticing boys, but her body hadn't responded to a man since she was fifteen. Men asked her out often, but she always turned them down flat, partly because she didn't feel she deserved to be happy and partly because she thought the part of her that could feel attraction and respond to a man's touch had been destroyed by her assault.

Apparently not.

Because just the feel of Fletcher's body surrounding hers had a needy flame licking inside her. She wanted to feel his lips on hers, wanted to feel his hands exploring her naked body, even wanted to feel him buried deep inside her.

Startled by this strange turn of events, Dahlia all but leaped from his hold and spun around to face him. She video called with her family every week, and they flew out to visit her at least a few times a year, but this was the first time she had seen Fletcher since he was shot right in front of her. Despite eight years passing, she would recognize him anywhere, he had the same piercing blue eyes, the same short-cropped blond hair, but his body … well, let's just say it was the stuff pantie melting fantasies were made of.

He was watching her with a weird look on his face, and embarrassed, she smoothed a hand down her simple white cotton blouse. Dahlia didn't like men to look at her body, so she usually kept it covered, today she had on the blouse and an ankle-length blue skirt, both were comfortable, and neither were going to make her the star of any male fantasies.

"You here to meet your new little niece?" Fletcher finally asked, breaking the uncomfortable—and unless she imagined things—sexually charged silence.

"Uh, yeah, I didn't want to, but my mom is really excited about becoming a grandmother, and I didn't want to let Abe down and not be here, so …" she trailed off and shrugged.

"Are you here to stay?"

"No," she said quickly, even the thought of that was enough to make her feel pressure on her chest. "I'm just here for an hour or two, and then I'm going back home."

He nodded, and she had to be mistaken when she thought she saw disappointment in his stunning blue eyes. "So, I hear you're starting the final year of your Doctor of Physical Therapy degree in the fall."

"Yep," she said, relaxing and giving him a genuine smile. She adored her job and felt like she was actually making a positive contribution to the world doing it. "I'm hoping to get a job at the veterans' rehab facility where I work after I graduate. I've been there for five years now, cleaning offices and helping out however I can, and I really hope I can stay there."

"You love your job, your whole face lights up when you talk about it," Fletcher said, and the smile he gave her made her insides go all gooey.

"I do love it, it's everything to me."

Sadness floated through his eyes, and then he was looking at her with that weird expression again. He lifted a hand, reached out to her, and let the backs of his knuckles trail impossibly softly over her cheek. Then he smiled and grasped her elbow. "Come on, let's go meet the newest member of the Black family."

Thoroughly confused as to what Fletcher was thinking, to what *she* was thinking, Dahlia allowed herself to be guided across the parking garage and into the elevator. Something with Fletcher felt different than it had before. She didn't know why but she did know she didn't like it—or maybe she liked it a little too much.

The sooner she got out of River's End, the better.

NOVEMBER 2ND

8:10 A.M.

And here Dahlia was back in River's End, just five months after her last visit.

"Stay safe."

"I will, I'll have an entire entourage of over-protective big brothers and cousins who I'm guessing aren't going to let me out of their sight," Dahlia assured her friend, wishing she was back in San Diego with her friend. Claire had just lived through a horrific ordeal and was struggling and she wanted to be there to support her friend.

But she couldn't be.

Because she'd had to come back here.

"They love you," her friend reminded her.

At least she had Logan.

"They do," Dahlia agreed, somewhat reluctantly. They had stood by her while she had struggled with PTSD and survivor's guilt, she loved them for it but didn't feel like she deserved their support.

"Keep me updated."

"I will. I'm sorry I had to leave you alone. Maybe you should call up those friends your man tried to set you up with."

"Yeah, maybe," Claire said vaguely, and Dahlia knew she wouldn't.

"I have to go, I'm about to rent a car."

"Okay, thanks for letting me know you arrived safely, I hope your brothers and the FBI can get this sorted out."

"Me too. Bye, Claire."

"Bye."

As she joined the car rental line, Dahlia rubbed her arms to ward off a chill. Coming back here was the last thing she had expected to happen. When she had driven away last time, so confused about Fletcher and what she felt for him, she had promised herself that nothing on this earth would make her come back.

Yet here she was again.

Only this time, she wasn't here to meet a new family member, she was here because someone had threatened her.

She still couldn't get that video out of her head. It had been three days since she received it and the first thing she had done was send a copy to her brother Abe, the Sheriff of River's End because she trusted him and was scared. A copy was sent to the local police department where she lived because she wasn't sure if the person who sent her the video was watching her, and another to the FBI because they had worked the case last time.

It was back.

The game.

RTK.

Rape. Torture. Kill.

After eight years, someone had decided to start playing again. As she'd already explained several times now she had no idea who, she'd thought everyone involved had been killed that day in the warehouse, but apparently not. There must have been someone else, someone who hadn't been hands-on, and for whatever reason that person had decided that now was the time to restart the game.

That was scary enough, but worse than that was how did they know about her? How did they know where she lived? How did they find her phone number?

No one but her family, her couple of friends, and her work had her number. She didn't even give it out to her doctor or dentist or gym, she didn't want people being able to contact her. She just wanted to be left alone.

But what she wanted didn't matter right now.

When she'd gotten the first video her brother, the cops, and the FBI, had all wanted her to get out of San Diego for a while, head back home to River's End where she would be safe, but her safety wasn't enough of a reason to get her to agree to come back here.

Theirs was though.

The girls.

The ones who had been lured in to play the next round of the game.

He'd sent her videos of three teenage girls, kept in cages eerily similar to the ones she and her friends had been locked in, told her it was too late to save them, but if she didn't want others to be taken then she had to come back to River's End.

It seemed someone wasn't happy she had survived the game and wanted to rectify that.

As soon as she knew that others were in danger if she stayed away, she immediately booked a flight. Much to the annoyance of law enforcement who once they knew she was in danger suddenly did a flip-flop and didn't want her coming back here.

Dahlia had made it clear that wasn't an option.

If she could do something to stop other teenage girls from living through the same horrors she, Alicia, and Brynn had then of course she was going to do it. What kind of person did they think she was?

She might be a coward, might have run from her family and their pity, the town and their blame, herself and her fears, but she would never turn her back on an innocent kid. So here she was, driving into town, desperately wishing she was anywhere else, not wanting to see her family but knowing there was no other option.

Not wanting to see Fletcher but knowing there was no other option.

Fletcher Harris.

The boy who had teased her mercilessly like an older brother had morphed into a man she had fantasized about as a teen. Back then, when she'd been young, and carefree, and innocent, she had dreamed about him being her first kiss, of him no longer looking at her as a child but as a woman. A sexy woman he wanted to take to bed. She'd had a whole fantasy worked out about how romantic it would be to lose her virginity to him.

Instead, that had been stolen from her on the dirty, concrete floor of a cage by a monster who planned to kill her or sell her when he was finished playing with her.

Since then there had only been one other guy. Not long after moving to San Diego, she had gone to a bar with the express purpose of picking up a random guy to go and have sex with. At the time, it had seemed like a vitally important part of moving on, proving to herself that she could have sex if she chose to.

It wasn't until it was done that she had realized it was a mistake.

The guy hadn't cared about her, had taken her roughly up against a wall in the back alley behind the bar. He hadn't bothered to make sure that she had received any pleasure, and once it was done, he'd left her out there with her skirt hiked up around her hips and her torn panties lying discarded on the ground.

Now she wished that she had waited for someone who could have made it special. In the five months since she had come here to meet her newborn niece, that someone suddenly had a face.

Fletcher's face.

She couldn't stop thinking about him and … he made her body feel things.

A kind of restless, needy desire that seemed to constantly hover low in her belly. More often than not, she dreamed about him making love to her, and a few times she'd even woken up on the verge of coming.

Part of her had wanted to touch herself, make her feel that

indescribable ecstasy that people were always talking about, but she was afraid.

Afraid to feel good.

Afraid to feel anything but the guilt she wore like an extra appendage.

Afraid that if she did it would mean letting go of Alicia and Brynn, and she couldn't do that.

Which meant that the most important part of her stay in River's End was keeping as much distance between herself and Fletcher as possible.

Her phone rang, and she answered it when she saw Abe's name on the screen.

"Hey, kid, you make your flight okay?" he asked.

While his calm voice soothed her fears a little, his use of the old nickname irritated her. "I'm not a kid anymore you know, I'm twenty-three and in my last year of studying. This time next year I'm going to be a fully qualified physical therapist, so I think it's time to stop acting like I'm still ten years old with pig-tails and braces."

If it was possible, she could almost hear his smile coming down the phone line, which only annoyed her more. She was always going to be just a kid to her big brothers … and to Fletcher.

Dream Fletcher might make love to her like she was the most beautiful thing in the world, but real life Fletcher no doubt still saw her as that same little girl he used to tease. Or worse as the broken, battered, traumatized girl in the cage who had gotten him shot.

"Sorry, almost-doctor Black," Abe drawled in a teasing voice, and she rolled her eyes and stuck out her tongue, glad he couldn't see her.

"Yes, I made my flight. It got in a little early, and it wasn't busy so I'm already in town. I'll be there in about ten minutes." Ten minutes wasn't long enough to get the hoard of nervous butterflies in her stomach under control. She didn't want to be here, she didn't want the past to be dredged back up. She didn't want more girls to suffer like she had. She didn't want to see Abe and her cousins and the new deputies.

And she definitely didn't want to see Fletcher.

Dealing with her dreams and the attraction she felt for him was hard enough when there was an entire country between them. How was she supposed to do it when she had to see him face to face?

She didn't want him stirring up these feelings, she didn't want him making her long for things that she shouldn't, and she didn't want him awakening a sensual side to herself that she didn't even know she had. She just wanted to live her life quietly, doing her best to make up for the mistakes that she'd made and the lives that those mistakes had cost.

The problem was that life didn't always give you what you wanted.

She was ten minutes away from seeing the man who had the power to completely disassemble her orderly little world and rebuild it into something she didn't feel that she deserved.

How could she fall in love, get married, have kids when Alicia and Brynn were buried in the ground?

Simple answer was she couldn't.

She didn't deserve happiness.

Didn't deserve a life filled with love.

Dahlia knew she would do well to remember that because she was about to face perhaps her biggest obstacle ever in one six-foot-three, blond, blue-eyed, too sexy for his own good man.

* * * * *

9:28 A.M.

Fletcher watched Abe as he talked on the phone to his baby

sister.

Dahlia Black.

She'd been a little terror as a child, an endless ball of energy who somehow managed to get into more trouble than her three older brothers combined. Underneath the energy had been a sweet girl who loved openly and with every fiber of her being.

Until one mistake had changed everything.

He remembered that day with crystal clear clarity that hadn't diminished over eight years. He and his best friend Theo Black had been home from their most recent tour in Afghanistan when Dahlia went missing. Dahlia's parents, Tatiana and Patrick, had been more a mother and father to him than his own parents had been. They'd practically raised him, and the looks on their faces when they realized their baby was gone and in trouble was seared into his mind's eye.

Seven days.

That was how long she was held before the FBI managed to get a lead on a dark web game where three young girls were taken, and people paid money to vote on which girl received which form of torture. The men placed bets on how they thought the voting would work out and had the chance to win money. There were also rumors that the girls who weren't killed as part of the game were eligible to be sold afterward.

In the end, they had arrived just minutes too late to save fifteen-year-old Dahlia from being raped, but they had managed to save her life and the life of one of her friends.

Only the Dahlia that had left that day, skipping school to go to an interview with what she innocently thought was a modeling agency, never returned.

While he had thought of her often over the last eight years, he hadn't laid eyes on her again until five months ago at the hospital when they both arrived to visit with the newest member of the Black family at the same time.

Gone was the skinny teenager, and in her place was a stunning woman.

One he hadn't been able to get out of his head ever since.

That day, he'd inadvertently startled her as he approached, and in an effort not to hurt her as she tried to fight off what she thought was an attacker, he had pulled her up against his chest.

The second he touched her he felt it.

Attraction.

Want.

Need.

Desire.

He'd wanted to kiss her, might very well have done it too if she hadn't sprung out of his arms and looked at him with a shocked expression.

Had she felt it too?

Getting involved with her was wrong on so many levels, one of which was that she was his best friend's baby sister, another that she had lived through a horrific ordeal which he knew she hadn't yet healed from.

She blamed herself, the whole family knew it. The problem was that they didn't know how to help her deal with it and come to accept that while, yes, she had made a mistake in defying her parents and going to that interview, it didn't mean that what had happened was her fault.

He did have one idea though.

"She on her way?" he asked as Abe hung up the phone.

"Her flight got in early so she'll be here in ten," Abe told them. The them being himself, Abe's cousins Will and Julian, Beau Caldwell, and Sydney Clark, who also happened to be recently engaged to Abe's brother Levi, a doctor at the local hospital. Levi and Theo were here as well. While they weren't cops, they were former military and determined to help. They were all sitting around the table in the conference room at the town's police station, it was all hands on deck to deal with this situation.

Ten minutes, that didn't give him long to convince everyone of his plan. “I think Dahlia should stay with me while she’s here,” he announced, no point in beating around the bush if she was going to be here soon.

Five Black faces frowned back at him. That was okay, he had known that Dahlia’s brothers and cousins were protective of her and would want her staying with one of them, especially considering this was only the second time in five years that she had set foot in River’s End.

“Hear me out,” he added quickly before he could get hit with a mass of protests. “We all know that Dahlia has unresolved issues about her assault, issues that she refuses to even address much less deal with. This is the first chance we’ve had since it happened to actually try to do something to help her. She’ll be back here, she can't hide like she did as a kid after it happened. I don’t think we can waste this opportunity because we might not get another.”

“What does that have to do with her staying with you?” Levi asked, not looking convinced.

“Well for starters, let’s be practical. Someone involved in the RTK game is alive and well and playing again. That someone has already targeted and threatened Dahlia. Despite knowing she’s playing right into this guy’s hand by coming back here, she’s here in town. She’s in danger. Abe has Meadow and Dawn’s safety to consider. Theo, you have Maggie who is six months pregnant to think about. Julian, you have Mia who is still recovering physically and emotionally from what happened last month. Will, you and Renee are still reconnecting, and given what happened to her and what’s going on now with Dahlia, you can't tell me it won't bring up some bad memories for her. Levi and Sydney, you guys just got engaged, and no way is she going to stay with Beau because she doesn’t know him. That leaves me.”

“Syd and I just got engaged, but that doesn’t mean we can't have Dahlia stay with us. Sydney is a cop, I’m former military, and a doctor which means I can help her deal with the trauma of being back here,” Levi protested.

"Yeah, maybe, but Dahlia's biggest issue is guilt. She blames herself for everything that happened, including her friends' deaths and me being shot." That gunshot wasn't his first, nor had it been his last, but he knew that Dahlia blamed herself for him being injured, and despite the fact that he thought he had been like another big brother to her back then, she had refused to see or speak to him after coming back home.

It had hurt at the time, even though he understood where she was coming from, but now he believed it was something they could use to their advantage. Finally break through Dahlia's walls and help her heal and move on.

"Dahlia blames herself for me getting shot. If I can spend some time around her, force her to see that I don't blame her, then maybe she can start to accept that the only person who ever blamed her for what happened was herself. It might not work, I know that, she's stubborn and she's hurting, and she's had eight years to convince herself that the whole thing was her fault. But this is the first time we've ever even stood a chance at convincing her to believe that she just made one small mistake and that it's way past time to forgive herself for it. Her staying with me gives us the best chance at making that happen, you guys going to blow that just because you're territorial about her?" He arched a challenging brow at Dahlia's brothers and cousins. It wasn't that he didn't understand their protectiveness when it came to her. They'd been protective of her even before she was assaulted. It was just that he knew in his gut that he was right.

And yeah, okay, maybe he had a few selfish reasons for wanting to keep her close too. Seeing her in that parking garage had made him see her in a whole new light. She was a woman now, a beautiful one, and she was smart, compassionate, and brave even if she disagreed with that.

She deserved happiness.

She deserved to move on.

She deserved to heal.

He didn't know what the future held for them, and he certainly wasn't going to push her into anything she didn't want or wasn't ready for, but he also wasn't walking away from her. If she had felt the same thing he had when he'd touched her then he wanted a chance to see if maybe there could be something good between them.

"All right." Abe nodded. "I don't like it, but I can see how your reasoning makes sense, and you could be right, maybe this is what Dahlia needs to finally accept that it wasn't her fault. So, Fletcher, you're on bodyguard duty. You go everywhere with her. We know he's here waiting for her to arrive so we have to assume that he's going to have eyes on her once she gets here. The rest of us will work on finding this guy and the missing girls, and Fletcher, you keep Dahlia safe."

He would.

He would keep Dahlia safe, protect her from anyone that tried to hurt her, and hopefully find a way to crack through her walls and protect her from herself.

* * * * *

10:42 A.M.

This was it.

Hiding wasn't an option, which was the only reason Dahlia squared her shoulders, steeled her spine, and climbed out of her rental car, parked in the street outside the police station.

Wishing she was anywhere but here, she walked up the steps of the building she had spent a lot of time at when she was a kid given that her dad was the Sheriff. She wasn't surprised that Abe had followed in their father's footsteps. All three of her brothers had always idolized him, and even though she was a really girly girl as a child, her parents had always been supportive of anything she had wanted to do. Her dad had always been down to dress up in sparkly skirts and brightly colored jewelry, to dance around to Disney songs, or have a make-up session.

She loved him so much. All of her family, her mom, and her brothers even though they'd been older and they hadn't been super close. They'd still made an effort with her, taken her for ice cream dates at the ice cream parlor or picnics in the forest. They'd taught her to ride a bike, how to ski, and how to drive. They'd been good brothers to her, spent more time with her than they had needed to, and never made her feel left out even though she was the baby and the only girl.

She wished … well, she wished too many things and none of them were pertinent to her reason for being back in River's End.

As soon as she walked through the station's front door a pretty brunette with a mass of wild brown curls, that she recognized as Poppy Devereaux, immediately hurried over. Poppy had moved to town with her parents when she was twelve and was just a few years older than Dahlia. She'd always liked the other woman and knew that she had met someone earlier in the year and that he had moved to town to be with her and joined the police department, working under Abe.

"Hi, Dahlia." Poppy greeted her with a warm smile but thankfully didn't try to hug her. Dahlia assumed it was because Abe had made sure to tell everyone about her dislike of physical contact, something she was eternally grateful for. It was hard enough being here, having to see people who she knew blamed her for Alicia and Brynn's deaths, without having to fake being okay with hugs and handshakes.

"Hi," she returned warily, trying to gauge what the other woman was thinking without making it too obvious.

"Everyone is waiting for you in the conference room. Can I get you something to eat? Or drink?"

There was no way her stomach was settled enough to consume anything right now so she shook her head. "No, thank you, I'd rather just get this over and done with."

"I understand," Poppy said, her smile still in place, and something in her tone said she did understand how hard this was for Dahlia to do. "You go straight on through, I know you know the way."

Thankful for the couple of moments to make sure she had it together, she ensured her calm and controlled mask was in place.

She could do this.

With a deep breath, she opened the door, and eight pairs of eyes immediately turned to look at her.

Trying not to let her panic show, she offered what she was sure was a brittle smile and walked toward the vacant chair Abe pulled out for her, steadfastly refusing to look in Fletcher's direction. He might not know it, but he had the power to crush what was left of her. She liked him, always had, and if she was a different person she probably would have already made a play for him, but she was who she was, and what would Fletcher see in someone broken like her?

"How was your flight?" Theo asked her.

"Fine," she replied, not wanting to waste time on small talk. "Can we just do this?" she asked, a slight wobble in her voice which she ruthlessly yanked under control. She couldn't afford to show any weakness right now or her over-protective big brothers and cousins would likely forcibly take her away and hide her somewhere where they knew she would be safe. But they didn't understand the guilt of knowing that more people had lost their lives because of her was enough to break her. She was only human, and she was already carrying as heavy a load as she could manage, anything else and she'd be crushed under the pressure.

"Course we can," Levi said, reaching out to very lightly brush his fingertips over her hands, which she had folded together and rested on the table.

"You've met Sydney, so the only one here you don't know yet is Beau," Abe said, gesturing at a man with dark blond hair and brown eyes sitting at the end of the table.

Next to Fletcher.

She chanced a quick glance his way and instantly knew it was a mistake. He was watching her closely, and there was something in his eyes that looked like … no, she had to be wrong, he couldn't be looking at her with interest. Sexual interest.

Sucking in a breath, she quickly averted her gaze and looked back at Beau. "Nice to meet you."

"Likewise, I've heard a lot about you and your childhood escapades," Beau said, giving her a warm smile.

Dahlia cracked a small smile that quickly melted away as she realized that Alicia was the one who had been by her side through all of those silly childish adventures, and then Brynn had joined them when she'd moved to town. Now wasn't the time to get distracted by that line of thought, so she turned to Abe. "So, ask me whatever you want to know."

"We need you to run through for us your communications with this guy," her oldest brother told her.

While she wanted to sigh and remind him that she had already gone through it with him, with the cops, with the FBI, she knew that it wouldn't do any good. She knew from firsthand experience that law enforcement liked to ask the same questions over and over and over again. So instead of complaining, she started talking, "Three days ago I received a message from an unknown number, there was a video and a short message that said the game was back on. The video showed three teenage girls who looked to be around fifteen, sitting in an empty warehouse in three cages just like Alicia, Brynn, and I were. Of course, I immediately called Abe to tell him what had happened because, well, he's my big brother and I trust him. He told me to call the local cops because if this guy had my phone number he could also have my address. I did, and then I also called the FBI because they were the ones who dealt with the game last time."

"You notice anyone watching you lately, kiddo?" Julian asked.

"She doesn't like being called kiddo anymore," Abe said with a teasing smile, trying to lighten the mood and it was weird to see her serious brother being the one to try to make this as easy as possible for her.

"Actually, I always hated that nickname," she said, making an effort because she knew the others were too. "And, no, Julian, I haven't noticed anyone watching me, but I don't know how he got my number, hardly anyone has it."

"He sent you more videos, right?" Will asked.

Dahlia nodded. "He sent another about twenty-four hours after that, and then another yesterday. The second one was like the first. It showed the three girls in their cages and said he wondered which one of them was going to end up … uh … raped … like me." She couldn't not shake when she said that word, it still felt as though it should have nothing to do with her.

Levi closed a hand around hers, and while she couldn't say his touch comforted her, it did help to ground her and she was able to hold it together. No way was she falling apart in front of all these strong, tough, military turned cop guys, even if five of them were related to her.

"The message yesterday said that if I didn't come back to River's End, he was going to keep killing girls," she said. "So, here I am." None of the people at the table looked very happy about that, but they would just have to suck it up. No way was she hiding away while more people died because of her. "I don't know what he wants from me, he hasn't said, but I guess sooner rather than later he'll tell me. I've sent all the messages to the FBI, and they're hoping that when he makes a play to grab me, or tells me to meet him somewhere, they can use that to catch him. They don't have any ideas who it could be, they thought they got everyone involved, and I don't remember anyone else who wasn't killed that day being there while they held us." The FBI had made her go through pictures of the dead men to confirm that there were none that she remembered who weren't amongst the deceased.

"We're in contact with the FBI and working this case with them. Since the missing girls are from town and he wants you back here, we're assuming they're somewhere close by so we will continue to run our investigation sharing anything we find with the FBI," Abe explained.

"I'm not here to get myself killed, I don't have a death wish, I'll be as safe and sensible as I can be, I won't take any risks, and I promise to do whatever you tell me to," Dahlia promised. "I'm assuming I'm going to be staying with one of you guys?" She looked from Abe to Levi, to Theo, to Will, to Julian, but none of them answered.

"Actually, you'll be staying with me," Fletcher spoke up.

Her mouth fell open.

Surely she'd misheard.

She couldn't imagine her ultra-protective big brothers and cousins allowing her to stay with anyone but one of them, even someone like Fletcher who was practically a member of the family.

"With Fletcher?" she repeated, looking to Abe for help, silently begging him to change that arrangement.

"We discussed it, and we decided it was the best option," Abe told her.

Best option for whom?

Certainly not for her. She was both swamped with guilt for almost getting Fletcher killed, and attracted to him, staying with him seemed more like a recipe for disaster.

* * * * *

3:36 P.M.

It was obvious that Dahlia wasn't pleased about this arrangement.

Fletcher glanced over at her. She was sitting in the passenger seat of his truck, tucked against the door with her arms were wrapped around her stomach, staring out the window. She hadn't said a word since they'd left the station and he was starting to second guess himself.

Maybe she would have been more comfortable staying with one of her brothers, one of her cousins, or with her parents. He'd thought that she needed to be pushed outside her comfort zone a little. They all hated that she was still suffering and he had been sure that he could be the one to help her finally move forward. Now he was worried that was his ego talking. It didn't matter who helped Dahlia find peace as long as she was finally able to forgive herself and find it.

He'd take her to her parents' house, let her decide which family member she felt the most comfortable staying with while she was in town.

No.

This was what she needed. His gut told him that he was on the right path and if he backed out now, she might really be lost to them forever. They all wanted her back, she didn't have to move here permanently, but he knew the entire Black family would love for her to come and visit, be comfortable going out around town, and find happiness and love wherever she lived.

She deserved everything in the world, and selfish or not, every time he looked at her, he found himself wanting to be the one to give it to her.

"We're here," he said as he pulled into the driveway.

Dahlia dragged in a breath and lifted her head to look at his house. "You bought the old Brady house," she said.

"About two years ago."

"It's a nice house, nice place to raise a family," she said softly before looking down at her hands clasped tightly in her lap. "Are you … involved with someone?"

Surprise had his mouth hanging open. Was she asking if he was involved to be polite, because she wondered if anyone else would be staying with them or because she was interested in him?

"Uh, no, I'm not involved," he said as he turned off the engine, unclipped his seatbelt, and shifted in his seat to study her. "No one else will be staying here with us, just you and me, I know you don't like being around strangers, and I wouldn't spring something like that on you when we got here."

"Oh, uh, yeah, good," Dahlia said, refusing to look at him.

Now he was definitely rethinking this decision. Why had he thought this was a good idea? Had he completely forgotten how he'd felt when he'd held her in the parking garage last summer? How perfect her curves had felt against him, how perfectly she'd tucked into his arms, how badly he'd wanted to kiss her?

This had disaster written all over it.

How was he going to resist her knowing she was sleeping in the room just down the hall, showering naked in his bathroom, spending every day glued to her side as her bodyguard?

No matter how badly he wanted her, he couldn't give in to those desires. Dahlia was vulnerable, she hadn't healed from her assault and near-death experience. The last thing she needed was him pawing all over her like some testosterone-fueled teenage boy. It didn't help that little Dahlia wasn't so little anymore, she'd grown into a beautiful and sexy woman and he so badly wanted to explore every inch of her creamy skin.

Ruthlessly shoving aside his attraction to the gorgeous woman who was going to be living in his house, he forced a smile and opened his door. "You sure you don't want to pop over to your parents' house to see them before you get settled in? Or we can go over later, maybe after dinner?"

A small shudder rippled through her, he wouldn't have noticed if he hadn't been watching her closely. "I don't want to see them today," she said quietly. The edge to her voice told him she was bracing herself for him to rebuke her for not wanting to rush straight over to see her parents.

Fletcher hated that.

Hated that she spent her entire life just waiting to be judged.

Sure, she had made a mistake but what kid hadn't done something stupid they wished they could take back? Why couldn't she see that she wasn't responsible for what happened to her or her friends, that no one—including her friends' families—blamed her for any of it?

"No worries, I'll grab your suitcase," he told her.

Surprised hazel eyes darted up to meet his and then she offered him a small smile of relief. Of thanks. Only he didn't want her thanks. She never *ever* had to thank him for supporting her, understanding her, and caring about her.

And he cared.

A whole lot more than he should, given she was his best friend's little sister.

Dahlia got out of the car and followed him across the front yard and up onto his porch. They both went inside, and even though he knew that whoever had lured her back here couldn't have known that she would be staying here, he stopped her in the doorway.

"Wait here while I check the place out just to make sure we're alone."

She paled but nodded and waited in the doorway while he quickly cleared the house and confirmed that no one was here. He'd taken a long, roundabout way from the precinct to here just in case anyone was following them. No one had been, but sooner or later this guy was going to make a move, and he intended to be ready to protect Dahlia when that happened.

"We're safe?" Dahlia asked when he returned.

"Yeah, sweetheart, we're safe," he assured her, longing to reach out and smooth the worry lines in her forehead. "You hungry?"

"No, not really."

Fletcher frowned. "You have to eat," he said firmly, "and you skipped lunch, if I had to guess you missed breakfast too."

A small smile quirked up one side of her mouth. "You got me.

I was too nervous," she admitted.

"I know, honey, but you're safe here. Your brothers, cousins, and the FBI will find this guy, and I'm not going to let anyone hurt you." He hoped she knew that he would lay down his life to keep her safe if it came down to it, just like he would have been prepared to sacrifice his life to save her that night eight years ago.

"I know you won't," she agreed, and the sincerity and absolute faith in her eyes hit him hard. Hit him deep. It seemed like the most important thing in the world that she knew with certainty that she was one hundred percent safe with him.

"How about I show you to your room and then I'll make us something to eat," he suggested.

Dahlia nodded, and he took her suitcase and led her up the stairs to the second floor. Dahlia was right, the house was a good family home, and he did one day hope to share it with a wife and kids. Downstairs there was an office, media room, games room, and a nice open plan living space. Upstairs were five bedrooms and three bathrooms. The master had its own at the front of the house, and then there were two Jack and Jill bathrooms servicing the other four bedrooms.

"This is my room," he said, pointing down to one end of the hall. "You can take whichever of the other four bedrooms you want. You'll have your own bathroom so you'll have plenty of privacy."

She looked at each of the four closed doors and then pointed to the room closest to his bedroom. "I'll take that one if it's okay," she said.

He had no doubt she'd chosen it because it was right next to his room and she knew she would feel safer with just a wall between them. On the other hand, he was thinking of how hard it would be, knowing that only one sheet of drywall separated him from the woman he couldn't get out of his head. Seemed like he better get used to little sleep and cold showers.

"It's fine," he said. "You go get your things settled and grab a shower, and I'll whip us up your favorite dinner."

"My favorite dinner?" she asked, arching a red brow. "As if you know my favorite foods."

"Mashed potatoes, corn on the cobb, and bread-crumbed fish fillets."

Dahlia just stared and then gave him a reluctant smile. "You're just full of surprises, aren't you?"

"Sweetheart, you have no idea." He gave her a teasing wink, then nudged her shoulder, ridiculously pleased when she didn't shy away from his touch. "Go get settled, take a shower or a bath if you want, and relax, I'm going to cook us dinner."

He was halfway down the stairs when she called out. "Fletcher?"

"Yeah?"

"Thank you. For having me here, for giving up your time to play bodyguard, it means a lot to me."

"You're welcome, Dahlia." As he headed for the kitchen, he prayed that Dahlia never learned just how glad he was to be the one who was here for her through this. Keeping Dahlia safe was no hardship, in fact it was the opposite. It was exactly what he wanted to be doing, exactly where he wanted to be.

NOVEMBER 3RD

3:14 A.M.

She was here.

Timothy hadn't been sure that Dahlia would return to River's End, she hadn't come back since leaving town five years ago.

He knew that because he lived in River's End.

He was the one who had targeted Dahlia and her friends. He'd been the one who wanted her to suffer. He had suggested her to his boss and been thrilled when the man had been enthralled by the pretty redhead and agreed to lure her in to play the game.

That night over eight years ago, he had been lucky that he wasn't in the warehouse with the others because no one had walked out alive besides Dahlia, her friend Brynn, her family, and most of the cops, although a few had been killed in the shootout.

One of the perks of being the IT guy was that he hadn't been hands-on with playing the game. He'd been the one who sat in the safety of a hotel room, running the web side of things, and besides the obvious relief of not having to worry about getting caught or captured, he also hadn't had to worry about actually hurting anyone.

The idea of raping someone, or shooting them, or torturing them sickened him.

Literally.

The first time he'd organized the live streaming of the RTK game, he'd thrown up all over himself and almost gotten himself killed. His boss had been furious, called him pathetic, and said if he wasn't man enough to be part of this, he would have to be eliminated.

After that, Timothy had made sure he toughened up.

Being brought into the fold had been a real boost to his severely lacking confidence, and he'd known too much for them to cut him free, which meant it was either stop looking at those girls as real human beings or get himself killed.

What choice was that?

Self-preservation won out every time so he had learned to harden his heart, and now he was in the ironic position of being the one who would execute the girls' sentences.

With a smile on his face, he drove out of town, comforted with the knowledge that somewhere in River's End, Dahlia Black was curled up asleep, hopefully dreaming of him.

After the game had been so dramatically ended, he hadn't known what to do. He'd packed up his laptop, made sure the hotel room was completely wiped clean so that should the FBI link it to the game there was no trace of him left behind, and then he'd run. Right back to the town he hated where he had been forced to pretend that he hadn't been participating in the abduction, torture, rape, and murder of dozens of teenage girls. Like he didn't have access to bank accounts holding tens of millions of dollars.

It had been difficult, but he'd done it. There wasn't anything he wouldn't have done to remain a free man. No way was he winding up in a jail cell. He knew what it was like to be locked up against your will, imprisoned even though you hadn't done anything to deserve it, and there was no way he was living out the rest of his life like a caged animal. And Timothy knew that if he was thrown back into a cage he would become like an animal, a shell of a human, empty, broken, desperate to see freedom, and unable to he would die a long, slow death.

That wouldn't be fair.

He'd done the wrong thing participating in those girls' deaths, he knew that, but he'd loved putting his computer skills to use, and the money had been the deciding factor. Who wouldn't take the opportunity to become a millionaire just by running a simple dark web website?

It was true what they said, money made the world go around, and anyone who thought otherwise was either stupid or naïve.

Timothy was neither, and now he'd paid his dues, bided his time, and was ready to finally claim victory.

To do that, he had to take out Dahlia Black.

She was the only surviving member of the game, the only person who *might* be able to identify him and turn him into the FBI. It had to be done, and while he would have preferred to do this by simply taking her out one time she was back in town, he'd been waiting for five years for that to happen, and the only time she'd come back was to spend about two hours in the hospital meeting her brother and town sheriff's newborn daughter.

So she really left him with no choice.

The game had to be restarted.

The game would be the lure.

And it had worked.

Dahlia was now back. She'd been swayed by the videos he'd sent her and the threat that the game would keep going until she came back here and sacrificed herself. Well, he hadn't outright said that she had to sacrifice herself, but what other reason could she think he would start the game and send her videos demanding she come back to her hometown?

Now he was going to have to go through with it.

He was going to have to kill these girls. It was the only way to keep Dahlia here, amp up the guilt until she had no choice but to offer herself as a lamb to the slaughter. The Black family were all former military, cops, doctors, and firefighters, protectors at heart, and they wouldn't make it easy for him to get to her. They would be circling around her, her own personal squad of bodyguards, and he knew she wouldn't be staying at the hotel or any of the nearby motels where she would be easy pickings, no, she'd be staying with one of her military buddies who would be on high alert for anything out of the ordinary.

Patience.

The key to this was patience.

And luckily, Timothy had been forced to learn the skill when he was a small boy. That was now going to be what saved him. As soon as he knew Dahlia was eliminated as a threat, then he could take his money and flee.

But before he could do that, he had to tend to the girls.

His stomach was queasy as he turned off the road onto a small dirt track that led to the shed he'd built out here just for this purpose. It wasn't as big as the warehouse that had been used last time, but it afforded him more privacy because, unlike the warehouse at the docks, out here on the outskirts of this small, sleepy town the chances of anyone stumbling upon his captives were virtually zero.

He wasn't looking forward to seeing the girls. He couldn't stand their sobbed pleas for mercy every time he came here to feed them and film another video. He really didn't have the stomach for this kind of work, and if he had known exactly what he was getting himself into when he had been recruited for the game, he might not have said yes.

No, he knew he would have said yes even if he'd known the details. He'd been too desperate for the money, too desperate for a way out of a bad situation, he would have done anything.

Hell, he had done anything.

He'd participated in teenage girls being abducted and killed—or sold—even if he hadn't ever laid a hand on any of them.

But there was no one to do the dirty work for him this time around. He had decided to use the game to lure in Dahlia. It wasn't about money this time, he wouldn't be taking bids or votes, he wouldn't be live streaming anything. This was just the only way he could think of to finally be free of the fear of incarceration so he could live his life.

Parking the car, he grabbed his cell phone, turned on the flashlight, and struggled to get his hands to stop shaking as he pulled out the keys to the padlock. Once inside, he shone the light around the large space. The three cages were over against one wall. Against the opposite one was a table with the things he needed to complete his goal. He didn't look at them, couldn't stand the sight of them right now, knowing he would have to use them on these girls sooner rather than later. He was already struggling to keep the contents of his stomach from coming out because of the smell. He'd left the girls buckets, one to use as a toilet and the other for cleaning themselves, and the stench in here was overwhelming.

As he flicked on the lights, three frightened sets of eyes looked back at him.

Timothy didn't want them to know how nervous he was, how much he hated what he would soon be doing to them because if they knew, he was sure they would find a way to use it against him. Pretending he was completely in control, emulating the man who had run the game before, Timothy set up the camera then faced his three prisoners.

"Okay, girls, it's time to make another video."

* * * * *

8:02 P.M.

She was up, showered, dressed, unpacked, and as settled into Fletcher's house as she was going to get, and it was only two minutes past eight in the morning.

Dahlia hadn't given much thought to her go back to River's End plan besides getting back here as quickly as she could so that no other girls got hurt on her behalf. Now that she was here, she had no idea what she would do with her time or how long she would be stuck here. She could keep up with her studies online, and she had more than enough practical experience that she wasn't worried she would get behind in the requirements she needed to finish her degree on time, but suddenly the day seemed very long with a lot of hours in it. Hours she had no idea how she was going to fill.

Was she supposed to just sit here at Fletcher's house all day, every day?

Because that was going to be a problem.

Going to sleep last night knowing he was just in the next room had left her all flustered and … turned on?

Wow.

That was a shocker if ever there was one.

She had always been attracted to Fletcher, always been interested in him, but he'd been six years older than her and thought she was nothing but Theo's baby sister. Then she'd been raped, and suddenly no man was attractive anymore. She had thought of him a lot over the last eight years, but she usually felt guilty about getting him shot and almost killed. He'd taken that Kevlar vest off for her so she wouldn't have to be naked and surrounded by men—both cops and her family—and that one moment of thoughtfulness had nearly ended his life.

Now that she had seen him again, the guilt was still there, but it was coated heavily in desire. She actually wanted him to touch her, to kiss her, to make love to her.

Unsettled by this new development, Dahlia knew she couldn't hide out in her bedroom forever, so she steeled herself and headed downstairs to the kitchen. Fletcher was in there, sitting at the table, dressed in a pair of low-slung jeans and a t-shirt that did little to hide his impressive muscles.

Why did he have to be so sexy?

Why did she have to notice that he was sexy?

He looked up at her and smiled when she walked into the kitchen. "What do you want for breakfast?"

"I'm … uh … not really hungry," she stammered. At least not

for food.

Whoa.

Where did that thought come from?

It was one thing to be attracted to Fletcher, to have dreamed about him last night, to wonder what it would be like to make love to him, it was another to be so blatant about it, even if it was only inside her head.

"You have to eat," Fletcher said reprovingly, standing and holding out a chair for her at the table. "What about oatmeal? It's a great way to start a cold day."

"I guess," she agreed. "Maybe with a little vanilla?"

"Sure thing."

While he bustled about the kitchen making her breakfast, Dahlia sat and watched him. He'd been so nice to her, letting her stay here. There'd been no angry words about the shooting. He'd made her dinner last night, then they'd watched a movie, sitting at opposite ends of the couch where she wouldn't be tempted to lean into him and soak up a little of his strength. Now here he was this morning, making her breakfast, still no angry words, and the nicer he was the more she hated herself.

"What do you want to do today?" Fletcher asked when he brought her a steaming bowl of oatmeal a few minutes later.

"Oh," she said, surprised, "I wasn't sure I was allowed to do much while I was here."

"This guy no doubt knows you're back here by now, no point in just sitting around the house. I won't let him hurt you." Fletcher's blue eyes were so serious as he joined her at the table.

"I know, I trust you," she said, and it was true. Dahlia trusted him just as much as she would have one of her brothers or cousins, and that thought rattled her. Attraction was one thing, but trust was different, it meant something, it ran deeper and was way more intimate than she was comfortable with.

"Good." He smiled at her like her trust meant something to him, and that rattled her even more. "We can go visit your folks."

"No, not yet," she said quickly. She wasn't ready to see them yet because she knew her mom was going to badger her about staying here, maybe even moving back here, and this time she didn't have a pre-booked flight to fend her off like she had when she came to meet baby Dawn.

Dahlia braced herself for what she was sure would be a reprimand for not wanting to go running straight to see her parents, especially given his history with his. Fletcher's dad had bailed on him, his mom, and little sister Florence when he was just a little boy, leaving the siblings to be raised by an alcoholic mother who worked as a stripper and spent more time worrying about the men she slept with than her children. The family had been poor, lived in a trailer without electricity and running water, and Fletcher had spent most of the time at her house. Her parents were basically his parents, and she knew that his loyalty was to them, not her.

"We could go out into the forest, maybe go kayaking, or take out my boat, or if you'd rather go hiking we could do that instead, maybe pack a picnic," Fletcher suggested smoothly, not missing a beat.

Surprised and relieved, she relaxed into her seat. "Yeah, that sounds nice," she agreed. She'd missed the forest. In San Diego, she spent a lot of time at the beach, she loved watching the waves and had learned how to surf, but it didn't have the same peace and tranquility for her that the forest did.

Before Fletcher could say anything else, her phone dinged with a message. Without thinking, Dahlia reached out to pick it up, her stomach dropping when she saw who it was from.

"Is it him?" Fletcher asked, coming to stand behind her, leaning over her shoulder as she opened the message and hit play on the video.

"Yes," she said shakily. The words accompanying the video should have clued her in to what was coming, but it wasn't until she saw a man dressed all in black, with a mask on, the same kind the men in the warehouse had worn, unlock the cage of one of the girls that it clicked.

"Don't watch this," Fletcher said, snatching the phone from her hand and moving away so she couldn't see what was about to happen.

But it didn't stop it from playing out in her head.

The man had been unzipping his pants as he walked toward the terrified girl.

He was going to rape her.

The little that she'd eaten surged in her stomach, and she shoved to her feet and just made it to the downstairs powder room before she threw up.

Cold and shaky, she dry retched for several minutes after emptying the contents of her stomach then managed to climb to her feet. Turning the cold tap on, she splashed water on her face and then scooped some into her mouth to rinse it out.

Wanting so badly to stay hidden away in here where she didn't have to see Fletcher and the pity she knew she was going to see on his face, Dahlia knew she couldn't do that. She had to know if he'd hurt the other two girls or if they were still alive, so she dried her face, straightened her back, and walked out to the kitchen.

As soon as he saw her, Fletcher ended the call he was on, walked to her, and wrapped his arms around her. Pulling her against his chest with one large hand cradling the back of her head, he urged her to tuck her face against his shoulder, his other hand keeping her snug in his embrace.

His surprising reaction hit her deep, made tears well up in her eyes, and she chewed on her lip to keep them in. For a moment she stood there in shock, arms hanging limply by her sides, stiff, and then it was like one of the barriers she'd built around herself to protect herself from more pain cracked and shattered, landing at her feet.

Dahlia curled her arms around Fletcher and held onto him tightly, pressing closer suddenly, weary down to her very bones.

She'd felt isolated for so long, so afraid of seeing the same blame in other people's eyes that she saw in her own, that she had locked herself down, running from the guilt that had nearly destroyed her. She had thought she was doing okay, that she had it together, that she didn't need anyone else, but in this moment, she knew how wrong she had been because right now, the thing she needed the most was just to be held.

* * * * *

1:51 P.M.

That was it.

He'd had enough.

Fletcher couldn't sit there and watch Dahlia close in on herself any longer. It was like being forced to watch her die slowly, and he couldn't stomach it for another second.

"Let's go out," he announced, standing up and already walking to grab his keys.

"I don't really feel like doing anything right now," Dahlia said, her tone and her eyes were dull. After receiving the video message, he'd called Abe and the FBI, forwarded the message onto them, then Dahlia had been forced to answer dozens of questions, most of which were variants of whether or not she recognized the man in the video. She'd answered the same every time, that she couldn't see enough of him to know if he'd been part of her abduction or not.

Sitting here dwelling on what had happened to the kidnapped girl in the video and no doubt reliving being subjected to the same fate wasn't doing Dahlia any good. He needed to get her mind off things for a while. She'd trusted him earlier to hold her and comfort her—he'd been surprised when she hadn't shoved out of his embrace, but it had meant a lot to him that she'd let him hold her, maybe more than it should—and he had to hope that she would trust him now as well.

Crossing the living room, he crouched in front of the chair by the window where Dahlia had spent most of the day curled up, and rested his hands on her knees. She jolted at the touch, her eyes flying to meet his, a mess of emotions tornadoing their way through them, but she didn't pull away from his touch. Progress. "Come on, Freckles, you can't just sit here. Replaying that video over and over in your head is going to destroy you. Let me take your mind off it even for just a few hours."

Dahlia studied him, and he wished he knew what was running through her head, wished he knew what to say or do to help her. While he couldn't undo the past, couldn't force her to forgive herself or block out the image of what had happened to that girl, he could distract her for a while, but she had to let him do it.

"I'm not sure I'm up to seeing anyone," she finally said.

"Not a problem. What I have in mind will be just the two of us."

Fear flashed through her face, and he didn't have to ask her to know that she wasn't afraid of him physically hurting her, she was afraid of this *thing* between them. She felt it too, he knew she did, just like she had that day in the hospital parking lot when Dawn was born. Fletcher had to fight back a smile, maybe his plan to try to help her let go wasn't as hopeless as it had at first seemed.

"I guess we can go do whatever you have planned," she agreed.

Relief washed over him, but he played it cool, patted her knee one more time then stood. "Go grab your coat."

Eyeing him with curiosity now, Dahlia stood and hurried up the stairs to her room while he collected his cell phone then shrugged into his coat and waited for Dahlia to come back down. She returned a minute later, dressed in jeans, a yellow sweater, and a gray coat. With a white knit cap covering her red hair, she looked both sweet and sexy. He'd always been a simple guy with simple tastes, he was more comfortable in jeans and a t-shirt out in the forest than he was all dressed up at a fancy restaurant.

"So, where are we going?" Dahlia asked as she followed him out to the car.

"You'll see when we get there, Freckles."

She made a face at the old nickname, one she'd hated as a kid, but she seemed more relaxed in the seat beside him than she had when he drove her to his place the day before. It didn't take long for them to leave the town behind, and he drove for another ten minutes before pulling off the road onto a small dirt track.

Although he could tell a million questions were running through Dahlia's head, she kept quiet, staring out the window at the pretty fall day. It was beautiful out here. Fletcher loved the country, he couldn't imagine trading the trees and the river and the nature that was everywhere you looked for the city's concrete jungle. Whenever he visited his sister Florence and her husband Eli, who lived in Manhattan, he couldn't wait to get away from all the cars, concrete, and people and back out here to this small town that he loved.

Parking the car close to the river, he met Dahlia's inquisitive gaze and just shot her a grin. She rolled her eyes at him but got out of the car and followed close behind when he started walking.

"I don't see anything out here," Dahlia said when they'd been walking for close to five minutes.

"Just the way I like it," he said.

He could feel her growing annoyance that he hadn't yet told her what he had planned, but he also felt that she had relaxed as much as she was capable of relaxing, and he knew that for the time being at least, she had forgotten about her reasons for being forced to return to her home town. Pleased with himself that he'd been able to distract her, Fletcher focused on his next goal, it wasn't enough for her to relax, he wanted her to have fun.

Reaching the place he'd brought her to, he walked along the short dock he'd built when he first moved back here, gesturing to the small canoe he had also built with his own two hands.

"Nothing more relaxing than being out on the water."

One side of Dahlia's mouth quirked up in a small smile as she looked at the canoe and the paddles resting inside it. "You made this, didn't you?"

"Yep."

"You were always good at making things out of wood. I remember for my eighth birthday you made me that dollhouse. I loved it and played with it every day for two years before I decided I was too old for dolls. And when I was twelve and a little obsessed with all things animals you made me that birdhouse, it was so pretty. I remember you carved patterns on the sides and the roof." Her hazel eyes grew sad. "And for my sixteenth birthday, you made me that jewelry box. I didn't want a birthday party or presents or cake, but my parents insisted on at least celebrating with my family. You were away serving, and so were Theo and Levi, Will and Julian too, but somehow you were able to make that for me. I cried when I opened it. I felt so bad about you getting shot because of me because you were being so sweet."

He was losing her back to the dark side and determined not to let that happen, Fletcher stepped closer, stooped, and kissed her forehead. "I wanted you to know that I was thinking about you." Deciding now wasn't the right time to address her guilt about him getting shot, he took her hand, pleased when her fingers curled around his, and led her down the dock, helping her into the canoe and then hopping in behind her. "You remember how to paddle?"

"Did you forget who my parents are?" she asked. "We did everything that exists related to being outdoors, so yes, of course I remember how to paddle a canoe."

It was a lovely day, cold, but the sky was blue, and the sun was shining, there was a gentle breeze that was cooler out on the water, and the trees framing either side of the river were a mixture of reds and yellows and browns that looked more like a painting than reality. They paddled in silence for a while. Fletcher could feel Dahlia's stress melting away as the beauty and tranquility of nature washed away everything else.

Wanting to bring back the sassy, fun-loving girl he remembered from their childhood, Fletcher angled the oar, scooped a small amount of the freezing river water, and quickly lifted it, flicking it at Dahlia.

When the icy water sloshed all over her, she spluttered and spun around, sending the canoe wobbling wildly, very nearly toppling over and sending them both plunging into the cold river. "You did that on purpose," she accused.

"Guilty," he said with a grin, flicking more water at her, getting her right in the face.

Dahlia's mouth hung open, and for a moment he thought she was about to lay into him, but then she laughed. A real, genuine laugh that hit him right in the heart, he wanted to hear that sound every day, didn't think he could ever get tired of it.

"I think you forget who I am, Fletcher Harris. I have three older military brothers and two older cousins who were practically my brothers, I know how to give as good as I get. You'll be sorry."

Scooping her hands through the water, instead of tossing it at him, she stood and let the water drop on his head. Cold seeped into him as the water drenched his head and dribbled down his face and the back of his neck. He reacted by reaching out an arm and curling it around Dahlia, pulling her over then twisting so she landed beneath him lying on the bottom of the canoe, and scooped up his own handful of water, pouring it straight onto her face.

She spluttered and squirmed, but giggled as she tried to swat his much larger body off hers. For a moment, it was like having the old Dahlia back, carefree, innocent, full of life. He wanted so badly to help her regain that part of herself and knew he would do everything within his power to make it happen.

"I'm going to get you back for that, Fletch," she shrieked, wriggling until she managed to get out of his hold. Completely uncaring that she was getting herself wet and that they were precariously close to tipping over the canoe, she grabbed another handful of water and this time aimed it right at his crotch when she threw it. The resulting cold of course made his manhood shrivel, but his attraction to the beautiful woman grinning at him had him fighting not to grow hard. The last thing he wanted was to scare Dahlia off when he was making progress with her.

He caught her as the boat rocked and she lost her balance, falling into him and sending them both toppling over. She landed on top of him, her soft body pressed closely against his. There was no fear in her eyes, nothing but a gratefulness that made him feel ten feet tall.

"Thank you, Fletch. This was exactly what I needed," Dahlia said softly.

"Anytime, Freckles."

NOVEMBER 4TH

9:23 A.M.

She didn't want to be doing this.

Strangely enough, Dahlia wished that instead of visiting her parents this morning she was hanging out with Fletcher.

Since she was fifteen, guilt had been a way of life for her, but the worst had been guilt over Fletcher getting shot. He'd been there to save her, been thoughtful enough to want to make sure she wasn't made more vulnerable by being carried out of that building naked, and it had nearly gotten him killed. It was why she had refused to see him afterward even though he was practically a part of her family, and now in a twist of fate, she would much rather stay with him than go and visit her own parents.

Something had shifted between her and Fletcher yesterday. His touch had comforted her rather than panicked her, and he'd actually been able to make her laugh and have fun and forget about the past and the present for a few hours.

"Relax, Freckles. We're only going to your parents' house, no one else will see you," Fletcher told her from the driver's seat, and he reached out and covered her hands—which were folded together in her lap—squeezing them reassuringly.

If only he knew.

It wasn't just the other residents of River's End that she knew blamed her for what happened, it was her own family too. How could they not? She'd been completely stupid and willfully disobedient. Her parents had told her that it was no doubt a scam, but she had been so sure that it wasn't that she had gone to the interview anyway.

And paid the price.

It would have been one thing if she was the only one to suffer, but she had dragged her best friends into it too.

Of course they blamed her.

She blamed herself.

It was why she had left and not come back. It was hard enough dealing with her own guilt. Having to deal with everyone else's emotions on a daily basis was quite simply too much. Staying here would end up killing her.

Which meant she had to keep her growing feelings for Fletcher locked down. As soon as this guy was caught and there was no longer a threat hanging over the teenage girls of River's End, she was going back home and never coming back here again. Not for anything.

"We're here," Fletcher announced as he parked the car in the driveway of the house she had grown up in. She hadn't stepped foot inside it since she graduated high school. Last summer when she'd visited, all she had done was go to the hospital to meet Dawn and congratulate Abe and Meadow.

The urge to get out of the car and turn around and run straight back to Fletcher's was strong. She was pretty sure that if she begged Fletcher to take her back to his place he would, but she had to do this, and she'd already put it off for two days now. May as well just get it over with.

"You look like you're about to walk into your execution," Fletcher said, falling into step beside her as she walked up the porch steps.

"That's what it feels like," Dahlia muttered.

Fletcher gave her a sad look like he hated that she was hurting and wished he could make it better. What he didn't know was that he actually did make it better just by walking beside her. Just by being there.

Dahlia knocked on the front door, and a moment later it was

opened, and she was dragged into her mother's arms. She returned the hug even though she didn't want it, and then allowed her father to hold her as well.

"You don't need to knock on the door, this will always be your home," Mom said as she dragged her through the hall and down to the kitchen.

Dahlia might have spent the first eighteen years of her life here, but this place didn't feel like her home anymore. Now all this place did was serve to remind her of what she'd had and what she'd lost. Growing up, she'd never been embarrassed by her parents like other kids were. She got annoyed with them when they enforced strict rules, but she had respected her dad who had served in the military before becoming the town sheriff, and she'd been so proud of her mom for stepping in for other kids in town when their parents weren't there for them. She'd loved her three big brothers and her cousins even if they had been older and saw her as nothing but the baby of the family. She'd had the perfect family, could have had the perfect life, but she'd let it slip through her fingers.

"I made all your favorites," Mom said as they entered the kitchen.

Dahlia took in all the food spread out over the counters, way more than she and her parents and Fletcher could eat. Being back here had her stomach spinning on a way too fast carousel, she wasn't sure she could keep anything down anyway. "Fletcher and I had breakfast before we came here," she said, hating the look of disappointment on her mom's face.

"Well, then, I guess we'll be having breakfast foods for dinner tonight," Mom said, a hopeful light in her eyes.

Dread pooled in Dahlia's stomach. Was her mom planning on springing a family dinner on her? She looked to Fletcher, but he simply shrugged and took a seat at the table, snagging a pancake on the way. Either he didn't know her mom's plans or he had no intention of helping her wiggle out of them.

"Mom, I wasn't planning on staying all day."

"You can go and come back tonight," Mom said.

"Who did you invite to dinner?" If everyone was coming then she wasn't, she didn't want to ruin her mom's plans, and she didn't want to be a brat and make a scene, it was just that she physically could not handle being around everyone all at once. It was too much. She could only deal with so much guilt at one time, and being with her entire family and their wives and fiancées, all of whom no doubt knew exactly how stupid she had been, was more than she could bear.

"Since you won't be in town long, I thought it would be lovely to have the whole family around for dinner. It's been so long since we've all sat around this table and shared a meal, not since you were twelve, before Theo and Fletcher enlisted." Her mom looked so hopeful, and Dahlia hated herself for having to dash that hope.

"I can't have dinner with everyone, Mom," she said simply.

"Sweetheart, it's only your family, we love you, and I know you don't believe it, but none of us blame you for what happened." Her mom's tone was pleading, and Dahlia's guilt surged. She was an awful daughter.

"Your mom would really love to have her whole family over for dinner, Dahlia, can't you please come just this one time," Dad said, meeting her gaze squarely, and she knew he wished that he could order her to come like he could have when she was young.

"Mom has enough family around, she doesn't need me too," Dahlia said desperately. Why couldn't they understand that she wasn't trying to be difficult? She just couldn't face everyone she had hurt all at once.

Mom frowned at her. "What do you mean I have enough family?"

"You have Abe, Levi, and Theo, and all your surrogate children. You have Fletcher." She waved a hand in his direction, hating that he was here to witness this near meltdown. "And you have Will and Julian, you have Poppy, and you have Meadow and Dawn, and Maggie, and Sydney, and Renee and Mia, isn't that enough? You don't need me." A powerful ache started in her heart, squeezing her chest so tight it was hard to breathe. It spread through her body until she had a headache pounding between her temples and she felt shaky and lightheaded. She couldn't do this. Couldn't be here. She was hurting the people she loved all over again. "Fletcher, I want to leave now," she said. Not bothering to wait for him, she spun around and bolted from the house.

Her parents had done nothing but love and support her, and she repaid them by hurting them.

They should just let her go, stop trying to help her, and accept that she couldn't be helped. She was doing the best she could to live her life with the weight of her mistakes on her shoulders, but it was clear she wasn't doing a very good job.

She wanted to leave, go back to her life where she didn't have to be confronted by the damage she had done to her entire family, but she was stuck here until the kidnapper was caught. Tears streamed down her cheeks, and she leaned against Fletcher's truck and buried her face in her hands. She was so ashamed of herself, she knew that her family wanted her to forgive herself, but she didn't know how. It wasn't like she enjoyed being consumed by guilt, but she didn't know how to make it stop.

Strong arms curled around her, drawing her into an embrace. Dahlia fought against Fletcher's hold, she didn't deserve his comfort. Couldn't he see that? She'd just devastated her mother because the very idea of a family dinner nearly shattered her.

Dahlia shoved at his chest, tried to break free of his arms, but he simply held on. He didn't say a word, didn't reprimand her, didn't tell her she had to forgive herself, didn't give her a string of consolations telling her everything would be okay when she knew it wouldn't.

He just held her.

Stood there and held onto her while she tried and failed to get free, then gave up and sunk down against him, letting him take her weight, soaking in the comfort he offered. Dahlia curled her hands into his shirt, pressed her face against his chest, and held on as a tsunami of tears burst out.

She might not deserve his support, but she was so grateful for it her heart felt almost painfully full.

* * * * *

6:36 P.M.

This was killing him.

Dahlia was slipping away again. He'd made progress with her out at the river, he'd gotten her to relax, even to laugh, and that lightness had remained even after they'd gone back to his place and had dinner, then spent the evening watching movies side by side on the couch.

Now they were right back where they had started.

Worse actually.

After she'd cried in his arms outside her parents' house, Fletcher had bundled her into his car and brought her back here where she had spent the remainder of the day curled up in a chair in his living room. He knew she was hurting, knew she blamed herself for what happened to her and her friends, knew she wasn't trying to hurt her family she just physically and emotionally couldn't deal with their pain on top of hers.

Fletcher ached to help her, but he didn't know how.

What he did know was that he wasn't letting her slip away from him. She'd burrowed inside him, gotten under his skin, was precariously close to reaching his heart, and he wasn't going to let her smother herself with the guilt he knew she carried with her every day.

"Hey, Freckles, dinner is ready," he said.

"Not hungry," came the muted reply.

That was what she'd said at lunchtime, this time he wasn't letting her wriggle out of eating. She was under a lot of stress, with her past being dragged back up and being back here, she needed to keep her strength up. "You need to eat, Freckles," he said, taking a chance by reaching out, taking her hand, and pulling her to her feet. "We'll go outside. I started a fire in the firepit, and it's quiet out there, peaceful, we don't have to talk, but you need to eat."

He expected resistance, maybe tears, maybe for her to go running upstairs, but instead she stared into his eyes, seemingly searching for something. Then she gave a small nod and allowed him to lead her into the kitchen. Not wanting to risk saying or doing anything to spook her, Fletcher picked up two bowls of mac and cheese and then led her out into his backyard. He'd started the fire hoping that he could convince her to eat out here with him before cooking dinner, and he hoped the tranquility of the evening could help Dahlia find some peace.

They ate in silence, but it was a companionable one. The wafting breeze and the crackling of the dancing flames seemed to soothe some of Dahlia's turmoil. He knew she was battling against herself, trying to find a way to live while simultaneously believing that she didn't deserve to. He wasn't sure how to convince her that making one small lapse in judgment—as a teenager who aren't known for their sound decision making—didn't mean she was to blame for what those men had done to her.

He did have an idea to distract her this evening though.

"You want to help me in my workshop for a while?" he asked, aiming for casual. If Dahlia knew how badly he wanted to help her, he had a feeling it would send her running for the hills. She didn't believe she deserved help, thought she had to suffer to make amends, and she would resist any and all attempts to convince her otherwise.

"Help you?" she asked, sounding mildly interested.

Pouncing on that he shot her a grin. "I'm busy working on a special project."

"Special project, huh?"

"Yep." He wouldn't be telling her what it was, it was something he'd decided to make as soon as he heard Dahlia was coming back here, something he knew she would love, and if he could get it done in time, he'd be giving it to her for Christmas. "So, you game?"

"I've never done any woodworking before," she said, doubt creeping into her tone.

"That's okay, I'll show you what to do, and you're a fast learner." Fletcher forced himself not to hold his breath as he waited for her answer. He wasn't ready to let her go yet. He enjoyed spending time with her, it was so different than when they'd been kids. Back then when they'd hung out, it was either doing things with her family or he and Theo being stuck babysitting her. Now he enjoyed her company, and he knew that if he could just convince her to forgive herself and lay the blame where it belonged, they could have so much fun together.

Thinking long-term was a bad idea.

Getting invested in any sort of relationship with Dahlia was a bad idea.

Unless he could convince her to let go of the guilt, she was out of here the second they caught the kidnapper, and this time he knew nothing was going to convince her to come back.

Dahlia looked behind them at the house, then over to his shed down in the back corner of the garden before returning her attention to the fire as she debated her options. Finally, she looked up at him, "I guess I could help you for a little while."

Relief washed over him. Not just that she had agreed to come and help him, but because in doing so she was slowly lowering her guard again. He was going to do whatever it took to get through those guards, scale the walls she'd built around herself, break through them if he had to, anything so long as he could help her set herself free.

"Great, let's go." He stood, took her bowl, and quickly ran them both inside, rinsing them out then stacking them in the dishwasher. When he got back outside, he found Dahlia right where he had left her. When she saw him approaching, she looked up with a confused expression.

"Why are you being so nice to me? You know my past, you know that I hurt my parents by leaving and not coming back, you love them, so why are you being nice to me? Is it pity?" The look on her face as she said the word made it quite clear what she thought about that option.

Knowing that it was because he cared about her, because he was developing feelings for her that he definitely should not have for his best friend's little sister, was only going to scare her off. So instead he told her the truth. "Because you deserve it. You deserve to have someone in your corner."

With that, he took her hand and towed her along behind him down the garden to his woodworking shed. He'd built it up slowly, adding more tools bit by bit as he started doing more and more woodworking. It had become more than just a hobby over the years. He'd started making wooden toys and selling them around town to earn a little extra money, that had led to him opening an online store to sell the toys, and now he made almost as much money selling them as he did from his full-time job as a deputy sheriff.

This project wasn't work-related though, it was personal.

"Wow, it's huge," Dahlia said as he turned on the light and she saw the large block of wood sitting in the center of the room. "I don't know how you take that and turn it into that," she said, indicating to the mostly finished toys sitting on benches ready to be painted.

"Well, you're going to learn."

"I don't want to mess it up," Dahlia said.

"You won't, we'll do it together," he assured her.

"Promise?"

Why did it feel like they weren't just talking about the woodworking right now? The desperation in her eyes stirred every single one of his protective instincts, and he couldn't stop his hand from reaching out to cup her cheek. "Promise."

She stared at him for a moment longer before offering a small smile. "Okay, then let's do this."

"Let's," he agreed. Fletcher went to the wall where his tools hung in a neatly organized rack, chose the correct size chisel for what they needed, and then picked up a hammer. "Okay, come stand over here," he directed, then moved in behind Dahlia. "Chisel in one hand, hammer in the other." She took the tools then waited for him to tell her what to do next. Instead of words, he took the hand holding the chisel, moved it slightly so she was holding it the right way, and then positioned it above the wood. Then he took the hammering hand and gently began to tap on the end of the chisel. "Like this, we're going to keep doing this, shaping the wood the way we want it."

Up close to her like this, Fletcher soaked in the feel of her body. She didn't fight against his gentle hold of her hands, didn't move her body away from his even though he was right up against her, and he had to fight to keep his mind focused on what they were doing, even though he couldn't deny how affected he was.

"What are we making?" she asked, a little breathily, and he knew she was affected by it too.

Something was growing between them, something he wasn't sure Dahlia wanted to acknowledge, but it was there regardless. He wanted her with a ferocity he had never felt for another woman. Given his childhood and how his mother spent her life, he'd always been cautious when it came to women, careful not to promise more than he was willing to give, but Dahlia made him want to surrender his very soul to her.

"You want to know what it is you're going to have to hang around, Freckles," he said. Since this was for her, he could hardly tell her that.

"Fletcher …"

"Shh," he admonished softly cutting her off, not wanting anything to ruin the moment. "I'm not asking you to make any promises, just be here with me, enjoy the calming process of making something with your hands, don't think, don't worry, don't feel, just be. Can you do that for me, Freckles?"

Dahlia shuddered out a breath and then she leaned back against him. "Yeah, I can do that. For you."

Adding those last two words eased a tightness in his chest that he hadn't even realized was there. This woman was strong, capable, and had survived what would crush most people, and even though she struggled every day she still got up, worked, went to school, and dedicated her life to helping injured vets.

But it didn't matter that he saw her as strong and compassionate. She had to see it in herself if she was going to have any chance at healing and finding peace.

As much as he wanted to fix this for her or show her the way to fix it herself, Fletcher knew it was time to take his own advice and just soak up the feel of Dahlia in his arms in this moment.

NOVEMBER 5TH

10:49 A.M.

Tatiana Black stared at the photo in her hands.

How much she missed seeing her daughter's smiling face.

The picture had been taken the Christmas before Dahlia was abducted, raped, and nearly murdered. She was sitting in front of the Christmas tree, grinning at the camera as she held up the Vendula London purse made to look like a little cake boutique that she had found on the internet and asked for as her gift that year. She looked so carefree, so relaxed, so happy, it was hard to believe that in less than three months their lives would be turned upside down.

She had been a military wife, knew what it was to worry about the safety of the man she loved. She had been a military mom, all three of her boys had served, and she knew what it was like to worry about the children she had carried inside her. But nothing had prepared her for the raw terror she'd felt when she realized that her baby girl was missing, and she might never get her back. Nothing had prepared her for seeing the look of utter desolation in her little girl's eyes.

That look had haunted her ever since.

Tatiana felt like she had failed her daughter. She didn't know how to help Dahlia, and she was slipping further and further away with each passing day.

Well, she wasn't going to lose her child.

She refused to let that happen.

Dahlia's words yesterday had cemented that in Tatiana's mind.

How her daughter could think that because she had stepped into mother some of the other kids in town who hadn't had anyone there to look out for them meant that Dahlia could be replaced she had no idea, but the very thought of her little girl feeling that way sickened her, and she was determined to put a stop to Dahlia's downward spiral before it got any worse.

Carrying a tray with a pot of coffee, several mugs, and a plate of homemade chocolate chip and macadamia nut cookies, she made her way into the dining room where the rest of her family were seated. Because this was important, she'd asked her oldest son Abe to work at her and Patrick's house today so everyone could be here. They were having an intervention of sorts.

Seated at the table was her family. Her three boys, two nephews, and Poppy Devereaux who had always been a part of their extended family but more so since her parents deaths earlier in the year, along with all of their partners. Fletcher's sister Florence Harris who Tatiana always wished she had been able to help more when the woman was a girl, and her husband Eli were also there. She loved each and every one of them, but as long as she didn't have her daughter, it felt like a piece of her was missing.

"Mom and I want to thank you all for coming, especially Florence and Eli for driving out from the city," Patrick said as she sat beside him. Her husband took her hand and squeezed it tightly. Their daughter's ordeal had brought them even closer, and she knew she couldn't have gotten through it without him by her side.

"Of course, we're happy to be here to try to help Dahlia," Florence said, waving off the thanks. "Besides, I'm six months pregnant and stuck on desk duty so I'd much rather be here helping my family." Florence rested a hand on her swollen stomach and smiled at Eli, the look on their faces reminding Tatiana of how excited and nervous she and Patrick had been when they were expecting baby number one.

So much had changed since then.

Dahlia had been a surprise. They'd thought they were finished with having babies, three young boys were more than enough to keep them busy, but then she'd found out she was pregnant, and when they learned she was having a girl, Tatiana had been thrilled. She adored all three of her boys, but she'd always secretly wished for a daughter. They'd been so close when Dahlia was young, but then she'd been kidnapped and started to withdraw, and no matter how hard she tried, she couldn't seem to bring her daughter back.

Drawing strength from her husband's long fingers wrapped around hers, Tatiana glanced around the table. "Fletcher is bringing her around for lunch in an hour, and we need to figure out what to say to her to get her to finally move on."

"Mom," Abe started seriously, "are you sure we can?"

"Of course," she said, believing it deep in her heart. Nothing on this earth would make her give up on her child.

"I don't know," Levi said doubtfully. "I mean, I want her to be able to forgive herself, but it's been eight years. Eight years of believing without a shadow of a doubt that she is to blame for what happened to her and her friends. How do we overcome that kind of self-conditioning?"

"Love," Tatiana said simply. Love was the only thing that could save her baby girl.

"She knows we love her," Theo said.

"Does she?" Tatiana asked because from where she was sitting, it didn't look like Dahlia did at all. "When she was here yesterday, she said something to me that made me wonder if she really does know how much we love her. She told me that I had enough surrogate kids to love and care about so I could just forget about her. If my daughter truly thinks that then she doesn't know how much I love her. How much we all love her," she added. Looking around the table at each member of her family, she knew that every single one of them would do whatever it took to prove to Dahlia that one innocent mistake didn't change how they saw her.

"She blames herself for what happened," Sydney said. She was the newest addition to the extended Black family, but her desire to get to know Dahlia even though she lived on the other side of the country had been unwavering. "I think we all understand that on some level. We need to convince her that we have all done things we regret, made mistakes that had unforeseen consequences, felt unlovable, had to battle to see ourselves as others see us instead of the way we see ourselves."

"I couldn't have said it better myself." Tatiana smiled at her soon-to-be daughter-in-law.

"How do we do that though?" Levi asked, slipping an arm around Sydney's shoulders. "We've all told her we love her. We've all told her that we don't blame her for anything that happened, that she just made a silly teenage mistake, that she needs to forgive herself. None of it seems to make a difference, she doesn't believe us."

"Because we all coddle her," Florence said. "She's the baby of the family, the only girl, she lived through something horrific, no one wants to say or do anything that is going to upset her, but maybe it's time to take the gloves off. Maybe it's time to push her to confront her feelings instead of trying to hide from them, maybe it's time to upset her. She's not a teenager anymore, she's a grown woman, she's smart and hardworking, she worked two jobs to put herself through college. She knows what she wants to do with her life, she's stronger than she gives herself credit for—stronger than *we* give her credit for—maybe it's time we start treating her as strong rather than babying her."

For a long moment, nobody said anything, and then Florence shrugged like she thought she'd said the wrong thing and opened her mouth to no doubt apologize and take it back. Tatiana quickly reached out to her. "Thank you, I think we all needed to hear that."

Florence smiled gratefully at her. "Every single person in this room has fought their own war, whether it be in the military, in the form of abuse, stalkers, grief, betrayal, serial killers, and every single one of us has come out the other side and managed to find love and our place in the world. Dahlia is every bit as strong as anyone sitting at this table, but she doesn't see it because we've all been more worried about protecting her feelings than we have in reminding her of her strength. All of us found someone to have our back, to catch us when we stumbled, to hold onto us when the storm felt too strong like it was going to blow us away." Florence held out her hand to Eli who took it, kissed it, then held it between his own. "Dahlia has that too, she just doesn't realize it. She has all of us, her family, we're not going anywhere, and we're not giving up on her."

"Never," Tatiana agreed as she turned in her chair to hug her husband. Her family was everything to her, she would do whatever it took for any one of them, including causing her daughter pain if it was the only thing that would break through Dahlia's protective shields and finally bring her back to them.

* * * * *

12:08 P.M.

Dahlia had a bad feeling about this.

Or maybe it was just guilt.

Either way, she knew for certain that she did not want to go to her parents' place for lunch today. She'd so much rather hang out at Fletcher's house where she felt safe or go and do something with him out in the forest where they wouldn't have to see anyone else.

Going to her parents' house, seeing them again after she knew she had hurt them by running out the day before, filled her with so much anxiety that she was picking at her thumbnail hard enough to make it bleed, something she hadn't done in years.

"It's going to be okay," Fletcher assured her as he parked the car then reached over to pry her hands apart. He pulled out a tissue from his glove compartment along with a small first aid kit. After cleaning away the blood, he put a Band-Aid around the torn skin and then lifted her hand to his mouth and very lightly touched his lips to her thumb.

The sweet and intimate gesture had her sucking in a breath, unable to block pictures flooding her mind of what it would be like to have his lips on hers. Somehow, over the last couple of days, she had gone from being consumed with guilt about him being shot while rescuing her and dreading the very thought of seeing him or hearing his voice, to craving the sense of security that he gave her.

How had that happened?

And so quickly.

"Come on, let's go in."

She shuddered at his words, dreading going in there. Yesterday she had proved once again that she was undeserving of the unwavering love and support her parents offered her. She meant what she had said, that her mother had enough surrogate kids—kids that deserved her love—that she should just forget about her.

Fletcher and Florence had battled abuse and poverty, Abe had been betrayed by the woman he'd intended to marry, Levi had loved and lost twice. Theo had battled self-destructive tendencies, Will and Julian had lost their mother young and dealt with their father's PTSD. Their partners were every bit as strong. Meadow had been abandoned and grown up in foster care, realizing too late that she had married a monster. Maggie had grown up with drug and alcohol abuse in her home, Sydney had suffered abuse, Renee had been sexually assaulted in her home, and Mia had dealt with not one but two stalkers. Her parents had opened their hearts and their homes to anyone who needed it.

They were the dream team in there.

Then there was her.

The very opposite of strength. She hadn't swum like the

others, when tragedy had struck her, she'd sunk.

Right to the very bottom of the ocean.

"It's going to be okay," Fletcher said as he undid her seatbelt and pulled her out of the car.

Dahlia got her first inkling that something was going on when Fletcher didn't head for the kitchen but instead to the formal dining room they usually only used for big family celebrations like Christmas, Easter, and birthdays.

Why would they be having lunch in there if it was just her, Fletcher, and her mom and dad?

She got her answer a second later when she walked into the room and saw everyone sitting around the large oak table.

Everyone.

All of her family was there, and they were all looking at her.

Without conscious thought Dahlia spun around, ready to make a run for it even if it meant running through town where everyone would see her. Fletcher moved, blocking her escape, and the apologetic look he gave her said he was in on this with the rest of them.

Betrayal sliced through her, she'd trusted him, felt safe with him, and he'd led her into an ambush.

"We're all here because we want to apologize to you," Mom said, and Dahlia spun around in surprise to find her mother standing watching her hesitantly.

"Apologize to me?" she asked, confused. Apologize for what?

"For letting you down," Dad replied, standing to wrap an arm around his wife's shoulders.

"You didn't let me down," she protested, still not really understanding what was going on here. What did her parents, siblings, or extended family have to be sorry about? They weren't the ones who had made a monumental mistake and been forced to watch others suffer the consequences.

"We did, sweetheart," Mom said, stepping closer. "We didn't handle what happened to you as well as we could have. All we cared about was easing your pain, making sure nothing ever hurt you again, and in doing that, we let you hide. We let you hide from the world and from yourself. The more you hid, the more your guilt grew, and the more it grew, the more you shut down and withdrew. If we had been stronger, we would have pushed you into going back to school, and if you did you would have seen that none of your friends, or the teachers, or anyone else in town blamed you for what happened. Alicia and Brynn's families didn't either."

"Of course they did," she said, fighting back tears. "How could they not? Alicia died because of me."

"Alicia died because she made the same teenage mistake that you did," Mom said, imploring her to believe.

"No." She didn't believe that, couldn't believe it.

"Yes, sweetheart. If we had made you go to the funeral you would have seen. Alicia's tombstone has your name on it. Loving daughter of Otis and Marcia Colton, favorite sister of Miles and Kaden Colton, lifelong best friend of Dahlia Black. That's what her parents chose to put on her gravestone."

Dahlia shook her head wildly. That couldn't be true.

"You needed to go back to school, you needed to go back to church, back to cheerleading, back to your life, but we let you hide away because the idea of you suffering even a drop more pain was enough to have us crumbling. We would have done anything to protect you, but in doing so, I think we made it worse." Her mom's eyes were so sad, so full of tears and love and Dahlia didn't think she could take it.

"At first we thought you just needed a little time to figure things out in your head, and then you would be ready to leave the house again," Dad told her. "But then days turned into weeks, and weeks into months, then months into years, and before we knew it, you had graduated and were leaving forever. We should have pushed you off the deep end, insisted you go to therapy, go back to school, try to rebuild your life. We didn't, and I think the more we let you hide, the more you doubted yourself and us."

"You tried to get me to go to counseling, I refused," she reminded them. Why were they so intent on taking part of the blame?

"We didn't try hard enough," Mom said. "You were only fifteen, we should have picked you up and carried you to the car and made you go and see a therapist. We let you down, Dahlia, let you think that we didn't believe you were strong enough to face the world, and I think that's why you've had trouble believing us when we say that we don't blame you for what happened."

This was too much.

They were being too nice to her.

Trying to shoulder some of the blame so she wouldn't have to do it.

She couldn't handle this.

The dam inside her broke.

"Stop," she shrieked, unable to stop tears from streaming down her cheeks. Seventeen pairs of apologetic eyes on her was enough to crush her. "Don't apologize to me. I knew that going to that interview was wrong and I chose to do it anyway."

"Because you were sweet, and innocent, and naïve, and believed what he told you," Abe countered.

"But I went, I disobeyed mom and dad and went anyway," she shot back.

"Like every other kid your age. All kids disobey their parents, you think Abe and Theo and I were perfect?" Levi demanded.

"Yes. You're all strong and smart and dedicated your lives to saving others."

"We made mistakes same as you did. Everyone makes mistakes, Dahlia, everyone," Theo said.

"Not mistakes that get other people killed," she said.

"Even mistakes like that," Will said. "Mistakes that hurt the people they care about."

"You know the thing about mistakes though?" Julian asked,

then continued without waiting for an answer. "You don't make them on purpose."

"You were a good kid, Dahlia, a sweet girl who cared about others, who wouldn't hurt a fly. You loved your family and your friends, and the decision you made that day to ditch school and go to that interview against our wishes doesn't have to define your entire life," Mom said desperately.

But it did.

It had changed everything.

Changed her.

"No one in this family ever blamed you for what happened, that was all in your head. No one in this town ever blamed you, that was all in your head. No one in Alicia or Brynn's families blamed you, that was all in your head too. The only person who ever put even an ounce of blame on your shoulders was you. Your guilt is killing you. It's preventing you from being happy, from having the life you deserve. You have to forgive yourself, Dahlia."

Her mother's words shattered the last of her barriers, and she sobbed as years' worth of pain and anguish came flooding out. Unable to stand in the room with the people who loved her enough to never turn their backs on her a second longer, Dahlia turned and fled.

* * * * *

12:40 P.M.

Finally she was letting go.

Dahlia sobbed then turned and ran from the room. When her mother started to go after her, Fletcher stopped her. "It's okay, I got her. There's one last thing that she needs to hear, and she needs to hear it from me."

Leaving her family behind, Fletcher headed outside where he

saw Dahlia flying across the yard. He took off after her and caught up to her about three houses down the street. Wrapping his arms around her, he pulled her back against his chest, expecting her to fight him but she didn't, she just stood there sobbing, breaking his heart a little more with each ragged breath she managed to drag in through her tears.

Scooping her up into his arms, Fletcher carried her back to his truck. She didn't curl into him and wrap her arms around his neck, but she also didn't struggle to get away from him, so he counted that as a win.

Buckling her into the car, he waved to her parents who were standing on the doorstep watching, and then climbed in and started driving back to his place. Dahlia was so close to finally setting herself free from her self-imposed prison of guilt, but there was one thing left she needed to let go of.

Him getting shot.

He knew how hard that had hit her, and he was the only one who could convince her that he would gladly have given his life that day to save hers. That was just who he was, and even though back then she had just been a fifteen-year-old kid while he'd been a twenty-one-year-old man, part of him had known that one day she would become something special to him.

When he reached his house he parked, rounded the car, and picked her up again. She was quiet now, no longer crying, but still curled in on herself. He knew she was feeling overwhelmed, shocked by both her family's apologies to her and from learning what was written on her friend's tombstone, but he also knew she was almost where she needed to be to move on.

Inside, he set her on her feet in the living room and immediately shrugged out of his shirt. He met her gaze squarely, not missing the flare of awareness in her pretty hazel eyes as she took in his naked torso and touched a finger to the scar just beneath his left shoulder.

"Do you know what this is?" he asked her.

The awareness was quickly replaced by guilt, and she nodded. "It's from the bullet that nearly killed you. You shouldn't have taken off your vest for me."

"But I did. Do you know why?"

"Because I was naked, had just been raped, and you wanted to cover me so that I wouldn't have to worry about all those cops there seeing me that way. You knew that I would be feeling vulnerable and you wanted to try to make it better for me, you knew that would help so you risked your life just to cover me with your t-shirt." Her voice hitched at the end, and he saw fresh tears pooling in her eyes.

"That was a *choice* that I made and one that I don't regret. You know who else made choices that day?"

"Yes. I did," she said softly, tear-drenched eyes downcast.

"Yes, you did." He stepped closer until he was right in her personal space, forcing her to tilt her head back to meet his steady gaze. "Who else made a choice that day?"

Dahlia shrugged fitfully, dropped her gaze, then lifted it again to meet his, silently begging him to tell her what she needed to hear.

Fletcher was only too happy to oblige.

Lifting a hand, he cupped her cheek and let his thumb caress her damp skin. "Alicia made the choice to go with you. Brynn made the choice to go with you. Joe Collins made the choice to kidnap teenage girls and use them for his own purposes to make money before either killing them or selling them. And so did every person who agreed to work with him. He made the choice to kill Alicia, to hurt Brynn, and to rape you. You seeing a pattern here, Freckles? Everyone gets to make their own choices in life, and while yes, yours unfortunately led to something horrific, that doesn't mean you're responsible for everything that happened, because everyone else made their choices too."

"Are … are you sure?" she asked. She looked so vulnerable standing before him with tear tracks down her pale cheeks, puffy and red-rimmed eyes, her entire body almost vibrating with the need to be reassured, to be convinced that it was okay to accept that she had played only a tiny role in what had happened.

"Sweetheart, I have never been more certain of anything in my entire life. Everyone made their choices, and everyone has to live with the consequences. Alicia and Brynn could have said no to going with you, and you wouldn't have gone on your own. So would you want them blamed for not telling you it was a bad idea?"

"No."

"That wouldn't be fair right? Because they couldn't have known what was going to happen, they were just kids, good kids who didn't quite realize how much evil there is in the world. Do you agree?" He needed her to say the words, to acknowledge them and the truth behind them."

"I guess."

"There's no guessing, Dahlia. Do you agree that it wouldn't be fair to blame Alicia and Brynn for agreeing to go with you or not?"

"I agree."

"So by process of elimination, it would also be unfair to blame you." He saw the doubt in her eyes, but he refused to let her give in to it. "Same rules apply, Freckles. Either I can blame all three of you for making a silly, childish mistake, or I can't blame any of you. There is no in between here. So what's your choice?"

"I … I suppose … I guess maybe I'm not completely to blame."

Fletcher mentally cheered at her admission, it was a small one but a place to start. "You're not to blame at all, only those men are. They're the monsters in this story, not you."

"Did Alicia's parents really put my name on her tombstone?"

"Yes." He'd been gone back overseas by the funeral, but he had gone to Alicia's grave to pay his respects when he returned to town.

"How come no one ever told me that?"

"Well, I couldn't because you wouldn't talk to me," he teased, smiling and winking so she'd know he was just joking.

"I couldn't face you, I thought you must blame me for nearly getting you killed because I blamed myself."

"I never blamed you, Dahlia. No one ever did. Do you think that you can believe that?" He all but held his breath as he waited for her answer. Fletcher knew it was now or never, if everything her family had told her today, everything he'd said to her wasn't enough to convince her to stop blaming herself and let go of the guilt then nothing ever would.

She searched his eyes, and then a giant shiver rippled through her, and she leaned into him. "I think I can work on believing you. I don't think it will be easy, but I think I can do it. If I'm not alone." She pulled back and looked up at him, her eyes searching his again but this time searching for something different. If she was looking to see if he was the one who would stand by her while she tried to undo eight years' worth of thinking then she would find it.

Slowly, he dipped his head, the hand on her cheek moved to curl around the nape of her neck, and he paused with his lips hovering above hers, giving her ample time to pull away if this wasn't what she wanted.

When she didn't move, he feathered his lips across hers.

Dahlia hummed her appreciation and melted into him. Her arms came up to slide around his ribs as she clung to him. Fletcher deepened the kiss, bringing her closer and taking control, slanting his head to get better access to her mouth as he kissed her like he'd wanted to ever since he'd seen her at the hospital.

She was beautiful, she was battling her demons with everything that she had, and she was putty in his hands right now. He feasted on her intoxicating taste, trying to infuse his support into every swipe of his tongue, every stroke of his fingers. He wanted this woman so badly his body felt like it was about to spontaneously combust.

Before things could get out of control, Fletcher reluctantly pulled away, framing her face between his hands, and pressing his lips to her forehead. "I'm so proud of you, Freckles."

She gave him a tremulous smile. "Thank you. For not giving up on me."

"Never," he vowed, realizing it was completely true as the word fell so easily from his lips. He was serious about her, under no illusions that she was magically going to get over what had happened, she had a long road ahead of her but he wanted to walk it with her.

"Never?" she repeated.

"Never," he echoed.

With a cry she launched at him, flinging her arms around his neck and when he lifted her feet off the floor, she wrapped her legs around his waist, as her mouth found his again and she started to kiss him.

* * * * *

1:13 P.M.

This was perfection.

Who knew kissing could be this beautiful?

Dahlia's only kisses had been awkward teenage ones, her fantasies had all featured the man currently holding her in his arms, but nothing could have prepared her for reality.

She wanted more.

She wanted all of him.

Maybe even the future.

That was a terrifying prospect for someone who had thought their future had already been stolen from them. But Fletcher gave her hope. He made her feel when her every instinct was to shut down immediately. He filled her body with a pleasant hum and made it want to burst into song.

"What are we doing, sweetheart?" he asked breathlessly.

"Make love to me." The words fell from her lips without conscious thought, but they were exactly what she wanted. She was eager to soak in every wonderful thing she knew without a shadow of a doubt that Fletcher could make her feel.

"Are you sure?" His blue eyes searched hers, and her stomach fluttered at the heat in his gaze while her heart swelled at the concern and protectiveness that was mingled there too.

"Would you be doing it out of pity?"

"No," he said firmly, and the desire in his eyes remained strong.

"Is this … thing … between us one-sided?" Dahlia wasn't sure that she could do one-off random sex again. She wanted to feel a connection with the person she was sharing her body with. The first time she hadn't wanted what the tuxedo man—who she had later learned was a man named Joe Collins—had done to her. The second time while she had willingly offered her body to the man from the bar, her heart hadn't been involved and she had regretted it as soon as it was done.

Third time was the charm.

"No, Freckles, this isn't one-sided," he said with an affectionate smile. While one arm remained beneath her bottom, holding her weight, he lifted his other hand to touch her face, stroke her hair, the wonder in his gaze saying that in some ways he was seeing her for the first time.

"I had a huge crush on you when I was younger, I hated that you only saw me as a kid."

"You were a kid," he reminded her, "and then in the blink of an eye you changed, you grew up. When I saw you the night Dawn was born you took my breath away. So beautiful." He whispered his lips across hers then touched his lips to every inch of her face. "So strong." His hand stroked the length of her spine and up again making her skin break out into a mass of goosebumps. "I haven't been able to stop thinking about you since. I dream about you, think about what it would be like to kiss you, touch you, and make love to you, and now you're here, and I'm holding you and kissing you, and it's even better than I imagined it would be. Has there been anyone since …"

"One." Embarrassed, she dropped her gaze, staring at the scar from the bullet wound she had inadvertently caused. "It was just after I left, I wanted to prove to myself I could do it. Sex. It was in an alley outside a bar. Up against the brick wall. It was … a mistake. I wish I had waited."

"Until what?" Fletcher asked.

"Until this. Until it was with someone I cared about, someone who cares about me, someone who can make it special."

A groan rattled through Fletcher's chest, and he grasped her chin and tilted her face up so he could kiss it again. "Baby, I'm going to make this something you'll never forget."

A smile lit her face. "I know you will. I always knew you would. I always dreamed you would be my first, only we're about five years later than I thought it would happen. I always dreamed that once I was eighteen—no longer a kid—that when you came home I would go round to your place, there'd be candles and rose petals, and I would be wearing sexy underwear, and I'd seduce you."

Fletcher watched her with an amused smile, then he set her on her feet and swatted her bottom. "Go on upstairs to my room, I'll be right up."

Confused, she headed for the stairs, wondering what Fletcher was up to.

"Oh, and, Freckles?"

"Yeah?"

"Don't take your clothes off. I want the pleasure of removing them myself." He winked at her and her cheeks heated as a spark of something she had never felt before ignited in her stomach.

Was this foreplay?

If it felt this good already, how was she going to feel when Fletcher was buried deep inside her?

Dahlia hurried up the stairs and walked into Fletcher's room. She hadn't been in it before but it was exactly what she'd expect, manly, simple, the walls were a light shade of gray, complimenting the dark wooden floorboards. The bed was a four-poster, the wood the same shade as the floorboards, and the bedding and curtains were both a dark blue.

Unsure what to do, Dahlia stood somewhat awkwardly in the middle of the room, waiting anxiously for Fletcher to join her. The longer she waited, the more nervous she became. What if she had a flashback to her assault? What if she couldn't perform the way the other women Fletcher had been with did? What if she was bad at sex?

Most of her doubts floated away when the door opened, and Fletcher walked in. In one hand he had a small bouquet of flowers that looked suspiciously like the ones she'd seen in Fletcher's neighbor Mrs. Hunter's front garden, and in the other he had five lit birthday candles.

Tears pricked her eyes. Could he get any sweeter?

"Best I could do at short notice. Next time you'll have your candles and rose petals," Fletcher said as he walked toward her.

"This is perfect," she told him. Never in her wildest dreams could she have pictured anything better than the shirtless man standing before her with a handful of freshly picked flowers and candles.

"Make a wish, sweetheart," he said as he crossed the room and held out the candles.

What more was there to wish for when she already had the man she had loved for most of her life standing before her offering her everything she had been too afraid to want. Was it greedy to wish for … she didn't finish the thought just quickly made her wish and blew out the candles.

"Don't move," Fletcher ordered as he walked over to the

dresser to put down the flowers and the candles, then he was stalking toward her with a look of raw male power on his face. "So pretty," he said as his hands framed her face and he kissed her.

Then his lips were moving, trailing a line of kisses down her neck, making her shiver with delightful anticipation. As he kissed her, his hands began to unbutton her shirt. When his fingers trailed across her bare stomach she moaned and lifted her hands to his shoulders, trying to urge him to … she wasn't even sure, she just knew she needed more.

"Patience, Freckles," he said on a chuckle. "I want this to be everything you deserve."

Forcing herself to be patient, Dahlia stood still while he eased her shirt off her shoulders, letting it slip down and land on the floor at their feet. Then he dropped to his knees before her, his mouth now almost even with her breasts, and the next thing she knew that sexy mouth had closed over her bra, taking her nipple between his lips and sucking on it.

Desire shot right from her breasts to between her legs, and she moaned, her head falling back. How had she not known that breasts were this sensitive?

Because she knew nothing about making love.

She was pretty sure Fletcher would be a good teacher though.

"More," she whimpered when he moved on to her other breast.

"Okay, baby," he said, taking pity on her and reaching around her ribs to unclip her bra. When his hot mouth closed over her bare nipple, Dahlia was pretty sure she almost came on the spot. He sucked, then the tip of his tongue would swirl around her pebbled nipple, and she was trembling so badly that she was sure if Fletcher removed his hands from her hips she would crumple to the floor.

She moaned a protest when he stopped his ministrations of her breasts, but then he was undoing her jeans and pushing them and her panties down her legs.

"They're not really sexy like the ones I always thought I would wear if I ever had you in the bedroom," she said, suddenly embarrassed by the plain white cotton panties.

"Sweetheart, it's not the underwear I'm interested in, it's what's underneath them," he said as he lifted one of her feet and yanked off her shoe. "Although maybe we can go shopping together and get you some sexy lingerie," he said with a wicked smile as he removed her other shoe.

"Oh, yeah," she agreed breathlessly. If Fletcher looked at her like this when she was wearing her regular clothes she could only imagine the look on his face if she dressed up for him.

His large hands cupped her backside, and he tugged her closer then buried his face between her legs. She would have been mortified at the idea of him putting his mouth on her, but she didn't have time, his tongue licked her, and she gasped, her hands flying to his shoulders so her knees didn't buckle.

He licked, he sucked, he took that little bundle of nerves that she had feared would never bring her the same pleasure other people talked about into his mouth and suckled, and she flew apart.

Pleasure rushed through her with the power of a hurricane, her entire body tingling as she panted, and moaned, and cried, and struggled to breathe. She'd never thought this could happen to her, but here she was feeling like her body had been possessed by something she couldn't even put into words, it was beyond that.

"Thank you," she said, throwing her arms around Fletcher and clinging to him as she wept.

"You don't ever need to thank me for that, sweetheart," he said, drawing her close, and she could feel his erection brushing against her thigh.

Dahlia didn't think, she just reached for him, stroking him through his pants, knowing that as amazing as what he had just done to her had been it wouldn't even compare to what she would feel with him inside her, their bodies joined as they shared that journey to bliss.

"We don't have to," Fletcher told her.

"I want to." More than she had ever wanted anything else in her life. Dahlia leaned over and touched her lips to the scar under his left shoulder, a kind of goodbye to the past, a vow to focus on the future, something she still had control over.

Fletcher stood, shucked out of his jeans, and went into his bathroom returning with a condom in his hand. "You want to do the honors?"

She licked her lips and took the small foil package from his hand. He was so big, and she half wondered how he was going to fit inside her. He jerked when she touched him, and she smiled, it was nice knowing that she had the power to bring this big, strong man to his knees just with her fingers.

Dahlia slid the condom down his impressive length and kissed him when he picked her up and carried her to the bed, laying her down and looking at her with raw appreciation in his blue eyes.

This was how it was supposed to be. The air crackling with anticipation and desire, need humming through her body, eager for more instead of fearing it.

"So gorgeous," Fletcher said as he stretched out over her, careful not to let his weight crush her.

His mouth claimed hers, one hand nudged between her legs, teasing her as she dragged him closer, needing to feel every single inch of him.

"Fletcher," she begged, she couldn't wait any longer.

He flipped them over so she was on top, his large hands spanned her waist as he set her on top of him. Dahlia positioned herself above him and already wound too tight to take this slow, took him inside her in one go. He was big, and she hadn't had sex in five years, there was a moment of burning as her body stretched to accommodate his size. Fletcher held still, waited until she was ready, then when he felt her relax he started to move, thrusting into her over and over again.

She started to move with him, meeting him thrust for thrust, so close to coming again she felt like she was balancing right on the very edge of a cliff. Fletcher reached between them and touched her hard little bud, and that was it, she burst into another universe, crying out her pleasure, as Fletcher didn't let up, thrusting and touching her and making it go on and on until she was one big, ball of indescribable pleasure.

When it finally faded, Dahlia sunk down against his hard chest, not willing to lose this contact with the man who was becoming increasingly important to her with every passing minute she spent in his company.

Fletcher didn't say anything, just wrapped his arms around her and held her close. "I got you, sweetheart," he murmured in her ear.

Yeah.

He really did.

And it felt amazing.

NOVEMBER 6TH

5:06 A.M.

He had to pull it together.

He was running out of time.

Timothy knew that he only had a small window of opportunity to get this done before it was too late and he would be going down in a ball of flames, yet he was panicking.

How was he going to do this?

It was one thing to rape that girl. He'd thought he wouldn't be able to do it, but when he'd touched her, he'd found himself growing hard and actually enjoyed it. Torturing the other girl had been harder, but he'd manned up and done it. But this …

This he wasn't sure he could do.

He knew he had to because it was the only way to further the plan, he needed to film the murders, send the video to Dahlia, so she knew that he was deadly serious when he moved onto phase two of the plan. Knowing what he had to do and actually doing it were two completely different things.

Timothy had never taken a life before, to be honest he got a little squeamish just killing a bug, so he legitimately wasn't sure how he would get this done. It was after five now. If he didn't move soon he would never get the bodies dumped without anyone seeing him. The sun would be up in less than ninety minutes, and the pre-dawn light would be here even sooner, time was quickly ticking away.

Too quickly.

Just go in there, he urged himself.

How hard could it be?

All he had to do was aim the gun and pull the trigger, it couldn't be all that hard. Then once he filmed the death of the first girl, he could turn off the camera, and then he could knock off the other two, then load the bodies into his van—one he had appropriated just for this purpose—and drive them somewhere to dump. He hadn't put a whole lot of thought into where he would leave the bodies, it didn't really matter, he wasn't hiding their deaths. Dahlia and the cops had the videos so they knew the girls were in danger and would be murdered, he just had to make sure he wasn't seen when he left them.

It all sounded so simple in his head, but the idea of pulling it off had him trembling.

Why had he thought this was a good idea?

If Dahlia hadn't turned him in by now then surely it was because she didn't know he had been involved. He should have just taken the money and run, disappeared eight years ago while no one had a clue that he had been part of the RTK game. He had wanted to, but he'd thought that if he suddenly ran then he might tip his hand, alert someone to the fact that he had been involved in what happened to three girls from his hometown. His father had already been suspicious of him and the fact that he suddenly had more cash than he should have working for the family business.

Timothy had never wanted to be a mechanic—he wasn't good with his hands unless they were flying over a keyboard, the only time he ever felt confident, in control, was when he was on his computer—never wanted to have to see his father at work as well as at home, never wanted to be part of his family either.

Who would?

A mother who spent more time away than she did at home, enjoying her career as the celebrated CEO of a multi-million dollar clothing company. Feeling emasculated as his wife earned more than he ever could in a hundred lifetimes as a humble small-town mechanic, his father had taken out his anger on the only available target.

His son.

An unplanned and unwanted child, his mother had made it clear early on she wasn't particularly interested in him. Even if she had known that his father was hitting him, and locking him in the closet so he could do his own thing and not be bothered with the kid he hadn't wanted and was stuck virtually raising alone, she likely wouldn't have done anything to stop it. The alternative was having to take him with her when she traveled and even as a child, he had known that she wouldn't want him cramping her lifestyle.

Embarrassed about his home life, Timothy found it hard to make friends, he kept to himself. When he was seven, his mother had given him a computer to keep him occupied when his father had been injured at work, and she had been forced to step in and look after him herself. From there, he had quickly taken an interest in coding, and over the years his skills had grown.

A plan to pay someone to kill his father had started forming in his mind, and he'd turned to the dark web, that had led him to the RTK gang, and because of that he now had more money sitting in bank accounts scattered across the globe than he could ever get through, even if he lived into his hundreds. More money than his mother had, but in order to finally be free of the town, and his family, he had to ensure that no one ever had cause to link anything to him.

Which meant eliminating Dahlia.

And to do that, he had to find a way to walk into the shed and kill those three girls.

It wasn't their fault, they had simply been an easy target when he'd spotted them walking alone one night. He needed three girls, and one of them had red hair reminding him of Dahlia.

Dahlia Black had been like the town's princess. Her father was the sheriff, and her mother ran several charities and took on some of the kids in town who for various reasons didn't have a stable mother figure and made them part of her extended family.

Never him though.

Was that because of Dahlia?

He was just a year older than her, they'd attended the same school, and he'd watched the bubbly, sassy, confident girl from afar, wishing that things could be different so he could ask her out.

Over time, he'd grown to resent her.

She had everything, perfect parents, brothers who were heroes to the people of River's End for their service in the military, a happy home with a mom and dad who adored her, lots of friends, and boys who were falling all over themselves for a chance to go on a date with her.

After he'd been pulled into the RTK gang, he had casually mentioned her one day, maybe some part of him hoping it would put her on his boss' radar, and it had. She'd been chosen, lured in, raped, and would have been killed or sold if her brothers hadn't come swooping in to save her.

Leaving him out in the cold again.

Only sixteen, he had no choice but to go back to his father, wait it out, then make his move when the time was right.

Well, the time was right now. She was here, tantalizingly within reach, as soon as these girls were dead she would realize how serious he was and when he offered her an ultimatum he knew what she would do.

She would come to him.

Then he could kill her and finally be free.

Not giving himself more time to dwell on what he was about to do, Timothy pulled the gun from his waistband. It felt heavy in his hand, unnervingly so, he was used to his fingertips being powerful behind the screen as they flew over a keyboard, deciding people's fate in the process, not holding a weapon capable of killing with the slightest of pressure from a single finger.

Storming through the door, he looked at the three terrified

faces watching his every move, went straight to the camera and switched it on, then he lifted his weapon, aimed it at the third girl's head and pulled the trigger.

She dropped.

The other two screamed, pleaded, and begged, but he blocked it out, this was hard enough without listening to their desperate cries for him not to hurt them, to let them go. He couldn't do that, surely they had to know that he couldn't.

He *had* to end their lives.

He *had* to eliminate the threat that leaving Dahlia alive would always have hanging over his head.

He *had* to because he needed to get out of here, he needed to be free, far away from the parents he loathed, free from the town that had never saved him, free to finally be the person he wanted to be.

Timothy switched off the camera, he didn't need to capture the other girls' deaths on film. He aimed at the girl in the middle, the one who reminded him of Dahlia, and fired. His hand shook so badly that he didn't get her straight between the eyes, his aim was a little low, the bullet penetrating through her cheek. She dropped to the floor, but her scream of agony had his stomach revolting.

Quickly he corrected his mistake then turned on the last girl who was sobbing so hard her entire body vibrated.

Why was she making this harder on him?

"I'm sorry," he said, then fired again, thankfully it was a clean kill this time.

Timothy let the gun clatter to the ground then dropped down to his knees beside it and vomited. It was done, but he would never forget what he had done in this room and what he had become.

* * * * *

8:52 A.M.

Fletcher just wanted to get it out there.

Not saying anything felt wrong, like he was hurting both Dahlia and her family.

Since they would soon be at the crime scene, he may as well just say it, he didn't know how well it was going to be received, but he wasn't ashamed of what he'd done. Yes, Dahlia was the baby sister of his best friend, and yes, she was vulnerable at the moment, but she had wanted him every bit as much as he had wanted her, and it had been anything but casual sex. He wasn't going to push Dahlia for more than she was ready to give, and they had a lot to work through, practical things like they lived on opposite sides of the country, as well as the psychological trauma of her assault which she was only beginning to deal with, coupled with the stress of someone determined to drag the past into the present. But they'd talked after sex yesterday, and both of them were interested in seeing what would happen between them.

Which meant he had to tell her brothers and cousins.

Her *extremely* protective older brothers and cousins.

Abe was driving, Will was riding shotgun, Julian was in the back with him and Theo who wasn't on call at the fire station today, and had decided to tag along. Because he'd wanted to check out the crime scene for himself, they'd left Dahlia at the precinct with Beau to watch over her. Her mom was going to stop by, and Fletcher knew the two needed some time to reconnect, Dahlia needed the support that only her mother could give her as much as she needed him. He hoped. Because he was quickly realizing that he would do anything for her.

"So, I have to tell you guys something," he announced.

Everyone looked at him, including Abe whose eyes met his in the rear vision mirror.

"What's up?" Theo asked.

May as well just say it. "Dahlia and I slept together."

Tension filled the car and for a second Fletcher wondered

whether Theo or Julian—or both—were going to hit him.

"What?" Abe ground out.

"We slept together, and it's not what you think. I … have feelings for her," he admitted. "Haven't been able to stop thinking about her since I saw her the night Dawn was born. It wasn't a one-time thing, we talked about it, and we're together. I'm not putting any pressure on her, she's completely in control, we'll take things as slowly or as fast as she wants. I'm serious about her and committed to seeing where things go, so it's only right that you guys know from the beginning."

Seconds ticked by and no one said anything, Fletcher fought the urge to fidget. He wasn't ten years old, he didn't need their approval, although he hoped they would give it, and he hadn't done anything wrong. He and Dahlia were two consenting adults, and what he felt for her he'd never felt for another woman.

Finally Abe's face broke into a grin, and Theo gave him a friendly slap on the back, Will and Julian were also smiling at him.

"She deserves a man like you," Theo said, giving his blessing. "I know that you'll take care of her, protect her, and make her smile. She needs that, someone who understands what happened to her and knows how to handle it."

"And it goes without saying that you break her heart we break you," Abe gave the obligatory warning, but from the smile that hadn't fallen from his lips he knew that Abe didn't see that happening. He was right, if anyone was getting a broken heart here, he thought it was more likely to be him. Still, he knew that if he hurt Dahlia, he would have to face the wrath of her big brothers and cousins.

"Understood," he acknowledged.

"Dahlia know you told us?" Will asked.

"Yes, no secrets between us, I want to do this right. I told her I would be telling you guys this morning, and she's going to tell her mom. She's nervous about how you guys will take the news, especially you, Theo, so make sure you put her worries to bed when we get back there."

"Will do," Theo assured him.

Fletcher relaxed, glad he'd made the right call in being upfront with Dahlia's family from the beginning. He really did want to do this right because he saw a future for the two of them. He could see himself falling in love with her, to be honest he was already pretty close. He respected her, was attracted to her, admired her, and could picture them sharing their lives.

Unfortunately, Abe was parking the car, and it was time to push thoughts of Dahlia from his mind. Everything he felt for her would become a moot point if they didn't find the man who had set his sights on her before he found her.

The five of them climbed out of the car and headed to where Sydney had cordoned off the area. She had been the one to respond to the call and been first on the scene. As soon as she had confirmed that the victims were who they thought, the rest of them had headed out here. They were about a mile north of town, and the killer had dumped the bodies of three teenage girls at the side of the road where a passing motorist had found them. The driver had seen a van screeching away as he approached, but unfortunately had been too far away to get a license plate or a make and model. Still knowing the killer was driving a van was better than nothing.

The three teenage girls were locals of River's End. They were sisters, fourteen-year-old Eden and sixteen-year-old Alinda Bennett, and Alinda's best friend, Opal McIntosh, who resembled a teenage Dahlia.

Now all three girls were lying, naked, at the side of the road. Dead because someone had decided to use them as pawns in a game that none of them yet quite understood. That he wanted Dahlia was clear, but why go to all this trouble to lure her back here, and why restart the game? How did he even know the details of the game? It wasn't like all the details had been made public, yet this guy seemed to know everything.

Fletcher approached the bodies that were lying strewn around, twisted at awkward angles, like their killer had literally just picked them up and thrown them there before driving away so he wouldn't be discovered. As predicted, the killer had sent the video of the first murder to Dahlia, only thankfully he had insisted on confiscating her phone, torturing herself by watching the videos was doing more harm to her already overloaded psyche and he wasn't going to watch her do that to herself any longer.

Shoving aside his anger at these innocent girls' lives being cut short, he forced himself to look more objectively at the bodies and immediately noticed something. "Look at this," he said, pointing to the body of the youngest girl. "He shot her twice, once through the cheek and then again between the eyes. There's blood on her hands like she held them to the wound on her cheek."

"A single bullet between the eyes killed the other two girls," Julian said.

"So he's a good, clean shot," Will added.

"Something made him mess up that shot," Abe said thoughtfully.

"No reports of gunshots, so wherever he holed himself up it's not somewhere he was worried about anyone stumbling upon, which means he wasn't interrupted while he was doing this. And it wasn't a form of torture because he'd already done that, this seems more like a mistake. Only thing I can think of that would make him mess up the shot was if his hands were unsteady," Fletcher said.

"You think he wasn't comfortable shooting them?" Will asked.

Fletcher shrugged. "In the video he seemed to know what he was doing, hit exactly what he aimed for, same thing he did with the other girl, this is the only one with two shots, and the kill shot was as clean as the others. If his hands were shaking it would have thrown his aim off slightly, made him miss. If they *were* shaking then maybe this is something he feels compelled to do rather than something he's doing for fun."

Abe nodded slowly as he took that in. "As far as we knew, everyone involved in the game was killed that day in the warehouse, if there was someone else involved then it was someone who wasn't hands-on."

"A computer guy maybe," Julian suggested. "He wouldn't have needed to be onsite, could have handled streaming and running the voting from a remote location."

"So this guy is the last one left, he waits for a chance to get to Dahlia, but she was tucked away afterward, too hard to get to her. He bides his time, decides he's waited enough, lures her back here, but this isn't about making money like the original game because the FBI hasn't been able to find anything linked to it on the dark web. This is purely about Dahlia. He doesn't get any pleasure from killing these girls, he used them because he thought it was the best way to get what he wanted," Fletcher said, fear running through his veins.

What he wanted was Dahlia.

And no way this guy went to all this trouble to give up. He wanted Dahlia dead, and he was willing to do things he didn't like to do it.

Until this guy was caught, Dahlia would never be safe.

* * * * *

9:33 A.M.

"My mom told me how you and Beau met," Dahlia said to Poppy. The two of them were hanging out in the conference room at the station while Beau worked in the office, and her brother, cousins, and Fletcher went to the crime scene. While part of her still felt like she owed it to those girls who had died to watch the video the killer sent of their murder, she was glad she had relented and let Fletcher take her phone, she didn't want more death seared into her mind's eye.

This morning, waking up next to Fletcher having spent the night sleeping in his arms she had felt a confidence she hadn't in a long time. Maybe there was some truth to what everyone had been telling her for years, that she wasn't to blame for what had happened. Fletcher was right, she had made choices, and she had to live with the consequences of those mistakes, but everyone else involved had made choices too.

The two of them had talked, and he'd told her that he wanted them to be a couple, that they could take things as slowly as she needed, but that he wanted a future with her when she was ready for it. Having his unwavering support over the past few days had her thinking that maybe it wasn't such a bad thing to let everyone else in, not shut them out.

So, she was doing her best to rectify that.

Poppy was practically a part of her family, and she knew her brothers thought of her as another little sister, so she was trying to get to know the other woman better.

Blue eyes twinkling, Poppy leaned in close, her whisper conspiratorial, "Can you keep a secret?"

"Yep."

"I'm pretty sure Beau is planning to prose on Thanksgiving. I overheard a conversation he was having with your dad about arrangements for the day, and I did a little snooping, and I found a drawing and a receipt for an engagement ring buried in a draw in his desk in our study."

"You went snooping?" she asked, amused.

"Hey, Beau is the one into the whole anticipation thing, I like to just jump on into things. I want to tell him that I know, but he's going to so much trouble to make it special, and I don't want to ruin it for him."

"My lips are sealed," Dahlia promised.

"I know they are." Poppy gave her a scrutinizing look. "You seem like you're doing better."

"I am," she agreed.

"Does it have anything to do with a certain blond who's built like a tank?" Poppy asked with a teasing smile.

Dahlia smiled back, and it felt so nice to smile again. "It might."

"I'm glad, you deserve it. Fletcher does too, I think you two make a great couple."

"Knock, knock," Mom said as she opened the door and breezed into the room. Although her smile was firmly in place, Dahlia could see the concern in her eyes. After the way she'd run out of the house in tears the day before it was no wonder her mom was worried about her.

"I'll let you two chat and go check in on my sexy boyfriend," Poppy said, shooting a secretive smile Dahlia's way, and she was happy that soon her new friend would be engaged to the man she loved and planning her wedding.

Maybe one day that would be her.

She knew without a shadow of a doubt that Fletcher would plan something really special if he ever proposed to her.

"Are you hungry?" Mom asked, holding up a basket that was no doubt full of homemade treats.

But Dahlia wasn't hungry for food, what she craved right now was a hug from her mom. Without answering, she stood and crossed the room, wrapping her arms around her mother and holding on tight.

After a moment of surprise at this uncharacteristic show of affection and willingness to allow another person to touch her, her mom's arms came around her, drawing her closer, and a sigh rattled through her mother's chest.

"I love you, sweetheart," Mom said as she started to cry.

Her mother's tears got her crying too, and Dahlia held on tighter, wishing she had allowed her mother to comfort her like this back then. But back then she hadn't been able to handle touch, she hadn't been ready, she'd coped the best way she could, and that had been by shutting everyone else out. Now she was trying hard to open that door back up.

"I love you, too," she said, burying her face against her mother's neck and clinging to her while she cried.

"My sweet baby girl, I was so afraid I had lost you forever." Mom stroked her hair as the two of them held onto each other and wept.

"I'm sorry," Dahlia cried, hating that she had hurt her parents with her inability to accept that what happened wasn't her fault.

"I don't want you to be sorry, sweetheart, you were hurting and scared, and I was never angry with you for shutting us out, you did what you had to do to survive, I just felt so guilty that I couldn't help you."

"No one could help me then," she assured her mother. It wasn't personal, she had always adored her parents, it was just she hadn't been in a place where she could hear what people were telling her, her feelings and emotions had been too raw.

"Then?" Mom asked, gently easing Dahlia back so she could see her face. "Does that mean you're ready to let us help you now?"

"Yes," she said, offering her mother a watery smile.

"Is that because of a certain blond built like a tank?" her mom asked, echoing Poppy's words from earlier, and Dahlia laughed.

"Yes, but not because he's built like a tank. I blamed myself for him getting shot, that and what happened to Alicia and Brynn were the worst things about the whole thing. I couldn't get Alicia's forgiveness, she was dead, and Brynn withdrew like I did, I wasn't ready to see her again and then it was too late, she'd taken her own life. I think I needed to hear from one of the three people I felt like my actions had hurt that they didn't blame me before I could start to believe it," Dahlia explained.

"And you believe it now?" Mom asked hopefully.

Not wanting to dash her mother's hopes but also wanting to be honest, Dahlia said, "I'm trying to. It's not easy because I believed for so long that the mistakes I had made were unforgivable. But I'm trying hard to accept that I did something stupid, but that those men were professionals, and that they chose to do what they did to us and all those other girls. I'm doing my best," she promised.

"I know you are, my sweet baby girl. And you have to know, Dahlia, that as much as I love your cousins, and Fletcher and Florence, and Meadow, Maggie, and Sydney, and Renee and Mia, and Poppy and Beau, and even your brothers, no one in this world can take the place of you. The wonderfully smart, sweet, and sassy daughter I hadn't planned on having but loved from the moment the doctor told me I was pregnant. You're my last little baby, and I didn't protect you, keep you safe, like I was supposed to."

"It wasn't your fault, Mom, you told me not to go, and I thought I knew better. You never gave up on me, even after I moved away you called every day, told me more times than I can count that I had to forgive myself, and yesterday you got my whole family together to tell me what I needed to hear even though you knew it would upset me. I love you, Mommy," she said then wrapped her arms around her mother's neck as another wave of tears hit her.

Mom guided her over to the couch in the corner and sat them both down, holding her and stroking her hair, rubbing circles on her back until the tears finally dried up. "I love you too, sweetheart, no matter how old you get, or how many people join our family, you will always be my special baby. And talking about people joining our family, can I safely assume that the blond tank is soon to be officially a Black family member?"

Dahlia's eyes grew wide. How had her mom known about her and Fletcher?

Mom laughed at the surprise on her face and smoothed a hand over her wet cheek. "I always suspected the two of you would end up together."

"You did?"

"You had a crush on him when you were a kid, and even though the timing wasn't right then, with him being six years older than you, I just had this feeling that the two of you were meant to be together. Same feeling I had about Theo and Maggie even though the two of them were only ever friends until the fire changed things."

Theo had saved Maggie's life last spring, and the two of them had ended up falling in love while she stayed with him as her hotel was rebuilt. Now the two of them were getting married at Christmas and expecting a baby in three months' time.

Dahlia had never really thought about having kids, it was kind of hard to when you couldn't stand a man's touch, and the thought of sex made you feel sick. But Fletcher had changed that. She'd known him all her life, felt comfortable around him, and when she realized he didn't blame her for him getting shot, it had allowed her feelings—all of them—to finally bubble to the surface.

"So, it's serious?" Mom asked.

"I think so. He's telling Abe and the others today, and he told me we could move things as slowly as I want to, but he's also been honest that he sees a future for us. Everything has been so messed up for so long, and it feels weird to finally start letting go. I know it won't be easy, but it seems a little less hard knowing that Fletcher will be beside me no matter what happens."

"You love him."

"I've always loved him. But now that love has to grow into something more, something real, I have to learn how to forgive myself, how to move forward so that I can give him what he needs. He deserves the best, and I want to be the best me I can be for him. For us," she corrected. For the first time since she was fifteen, she wanted to have a full life, not just a job she loved, but friends and her family, and a future with the man who had always held her heart in his hands by her side.

* * * * *

7:24 P.M.

"Where are we going?" Dahlia asked from the passenger seat of his car.

"You'll see when we get there," Fletcher replied.

"We're doing that again are we?" she asked but didn't sound annoyed in the least. She'd been so much more relaxed today, more like the old Dahlia he remembered. He felt good knowing that he'd been able to help her start moving on from the past, but also placed the praise for that where it belonged—at Dahlia's feet. She was the one working hard to let go of eight years' worth of guilt, and he was so proud of her for it.

"Sweetheart, being with me is going to be full of surprises," he said with a grin.

"So I'm learning." She returned his smile, but it was the warm affection in her eyes that stirred up all sorts of things inside him. Protectiveness was there, he wanted to keep her safe from this killer, and also from herself and the guilt she made herself carry, and there was attraction and desire as well, Dahlia was a beautiful woman. But it was the way she curled around his heart that he liked the best. The way he had grown up with his dad abandoning them, and his mom always drunk or jumping from man to man, then there was what had happened to his sister, it had tainted his view of the world and love. Something even the example of the Blacks and how they loved each other unconditionally couldn't completely undo.

But this woman, smiling at him and the adoration on her face, had the power to make him believe in all of it, love, marriage, families, fairytale endings, and soulmates.

Reaching over, Fletcher took her hand and laced their fingers together. "I think we both have a lot to learn about each other."

"I'm … I'm excited about that," Dahlia said like she couldn't quite believe it.

"I'm glad." He squeezed her hand then returned to the wheel as he parked the car. "We're here."

"The church?" she asked, confused, then gazed over to the side and he saw her eyes widen with understanding. "The cemetery."

"I thought you might like to come and say goodbye to your friend and your guilt," he explained, nervous now they were here. He'd trusted his gut in bringing her here, the same way he had in insisting that she stay with him while she was in town, but now that he had to see her reaction to his idea, he was worried he had made a mistake.

She sucked in a breath, and Fletcher was sure she was about to start crying and ask him to take her home, but then she fumbled with her seatbelt, ripped it off, and threw herself across the center console and into his arms. "How do you do it?" she asked.

"Do what?"

"Know exactly what I need before I even know it?"

"I trust my gut, and so far it hasn't led me wrong where you've been concerned."

"Thank you." She squeezed him hard and then pressed her lips to his.

"Do you want me to come with you or wait in the car?"

"I want you to come. If you don't mind," she added.

"Not at all."

Fletcher rounded the car and opened her door for her, taking her hand when she got out. As they walked in silence through the River's End graveyard, Dahlia leaned over to rest her head against his shoulder, and he wrapped an arm around her shoulders and pulled her close.

"My mom said she told me about the gravestone back when Alicia's family had it made for her funeral. I guess I blocked it out, I don't think I was ready then to hear that other people didn't blame me. I blamed myself, and it just seemed like everyone else should too," Dahlia explained.

"But now you're ready to hear it."

"Yeah, I am. I just wish it hadn't taken me eight years to get to this point."

"The timing had to be right, and there's no timeline for dealing with a trauma like the one you experienced. I'm just glad that now you're ready to be happy because you deserve that, Freckles, you deserve all the happiness in the world."

"I'm happy when I'm with you," she whispered, then leaned up to kiss his cheek.

"I'm glad." He captured her chin with his forefinger and thumb and tilted her face up so he could kiss her properly. "This is Alicia's grave."

Dahlia nodded and dropped to her knees beside it, her fingertips tracing the lettering on the stone. "I'm sorry it took me so long to come here. I … I wasn't ready before now. Brynn, she couldn't cope with what happened and she ended her life, but you probably know that already. I'm … doing okay. You won't believe it, but Fletcher finally stopped looking at me as just Theo's baby sister." She looked over her shoulder to shoot him a grin. "I'm so sorry about everything that happened, and I'm always going to feel a little guilty about it, but I think I'm ready to move on. I won't ever forget you, Alicia. I'm sorry I got us into that mess, but I'll forever be grateful to have had you as a best friend. I miss you, and I always will. Goodbye, Alicia."

Touching a kiss to her fingertips, Dahlia pressed it to the gravestone where her name was carved, then she stood, dusting off her knees, and when he held his arms open, she stepped into his embrace. They stood that way for several minutes, cocooned in Fletcher's arms as he tried to absorb as much of her pain as he could.

"Thank you for bringing me here," she said, her voice muffled against his chest.

"You're welcome. You ready to go home?"

"I'm ready."

Fletcher tucked her against him as they walked back to his car, and they sat in silence as he drove back to his place. Dahlia seemed lost in thought, but she didn't appear to be overly upset by the visit which was good because he had something special planned for her when they got home.

"You hungry?" he asked once they got to his place and he led her up to the front door.

"Surprisingly, given how much food my mom brought when she hung out at the precinct with me today, I am."

"Perfect, because I have dinner prepared and ready to go." Well, he'd called Maggie and asked her to drop off something from the restaurant that was part of her hotel. He opened the door and then stepped back to let Dahlia go first, excited for her to see the surprise he had for her.

"Oh," she gasped as she stepped inside the house. "Fletcher … it's magical."

Dahlia walked further into the house then spun in a slow circle. There were red rose petals scattered all over the floor, and hundreds of flickering candles filled every surface. It had cost a small fortune buying so many candles and petals, but it was worth it to see the look on Dahlia's face as she realized he'd remembered her teenage fantasy about how their first time would go.

"You better thank your sisters-in-law, they're the ones who had to light all these candles," he teased.

"I will, but definitely not the same way I intend to thank you. Dinner can keep, I want to start with dessert." She stalked toward him like a stunning hunter ready to devour her prey, and he couldn't wait to be devoured. Her hands went straight to his zipper, and once she had it undone she wriggled her small hands inside his boxers and took hold of him.

"How about we take this to the bedroom, so I can feast on you first," he suggested because if she kept that up it wasn't going to take him long to come.

"No, I want to touch you. I want to show you how much everything you've done for me means to me." There was more to it than that. He could see in her eyes that she needed to be in control, wanted to be the one to lead things tonight, and he was happy to oblige her—anything to make her smile.

"Okay, then how about we get rid of these." He shoved his jeans and boxers down his legs, pulled his sweater over his head, and then stood before her naked. The way her eyes traveled over his body, the raw appreciation on her face, had him growing almost painfully hard.

Then his sexy little redhead stepped up close, took his face between her hands, and kissed him. Her fingertips trailed along his torso, tracing the lines of each sculpted muscle as she worked her way slowly lower. He knew she was taking her time on purpose, wanting to make him wait, but she didn't know that he would gladly wait for her forever.

When she finally reached his hard length and curled those sexy little fingers around him, her gaze darted up and she gave him a sultry smile.

Fletcher groaned and flexed his fingers before curling them into fists so he didn't grab her and rip her clothes off, throwing her down on the couch before burying himself inside her. Dahlia wanted this—needed it—and he would let her have it, but as soon as she was done, it was his turn.

She took her time, stroking her fingertips lightly up and down his length before wrapping her hand around him again and squeezing. Unable to remain passive any longer, Fletcher curled a hand around the back of her neck and crushed his mouth to hers. Dahlia groaned, and her hand began to move faster, squeezing tighter, and a flame of pleasure lit in his groin, firing up through his spine and splintering out through his body as he came harder than he had in his life.

Dahlia was grinning up at him. "Watching your face when you came, knowing I unraveled you like that, it was … hot."

Fletcher groaned again. "My turn," he said as he stripped her clothes off, then scooped her up and carried her up the stairs and into his bedroom, where there were more rose petals and candles. The need to claim her in his bed, make her his, imprint her on his heart and his soul, was so strong he almost couldn't wait.

In the bedroom, he laid her down, stretched out on top of her, and immediately his fingers found their way between her legs. She was already wet, and he slid a finger inside her heat, stroking her deep and loving the way she moaned and tilted her head back, her eyes falling closed. He added another finger, stretched her, stroked her, curled his hand around so he could get that spot inside her that would shatter her into a million pieces as his thumb attended to her swollen little bud. He kissed her neck, her chest, her breasts until she was writhing beneath him, desperate for release.

"Look at me, sweetheart," he commanded.

Her eyes opened, heavy with desire, and he increased the pressure on her little bundle of nerves, and she came, crying out his name, as her internal muscles clamped around his fingers. He drew it out for her for as long as he could, and when she was done, he withdrew his hand and reached for the condom he'd left on the nightstand.

"No," she said, stopping him. "I want to feel all of you. I'm clean and on the pill."

"I'm clean too," he said. "You sure?"

"Positive."

He'd never done this before, never had sex without protection, and the thought of feeling every inch of her with nothing between them had his hard length jerking in eager anticipation. Last night they'd done it with her on top, he hadn't wanted her to panic, but tonight he wanted to be the one in control.

Watching her carefully for any signs that she was being

triggered, he prodded her entrance. Far from looking concerned, Dahlia moaned, her hips lifting off the bed, begging him without words to hurry up and get inside her.

Happy to oblige, Fletcher thrust into her, burying himself into her heat. Dahlia hummed her pleasure, her eyes closing, her hands coming up to curl around his shoulders, her nails digging into his skin, and he started to move.

He watched her face, the pleasure, the hunger that morphed into desperation as her body climbed closer to release.

"Watch me, baby," he ordered. "I want to see your eyes as you come."

She lifted her lids, locked her gaze on his, and met each thrust, and when he adjusted his position a little her lips parted as her world splintered into pleasure.

"Fletcher," she gasped, tightening her hold on him as her body trembled beneath him with the force of her orgasm. Only once he'd watched her find her release did he allow himself to find his own, and again it barreled into him, stealing his breath with its force.

Gathering her close, he rolled them to their sides and tucked her head under his chin, holding onto the most precious thing he'd ever been given, knowing without a shadow of a doubt that he could never give her up, she was his forever.

NOVEMBER 7TH

7:56 A.M.

"What do you want on your toast?" Dahlia called out when she heard Fletcher coming down the stairs. Last night has been so amazing, not just the sex, but that he'd arranged to have all those candles and rose petals for her and the dinner they had eventually had to heat in the microwave once they were finally able to drag themselves out of bed had been some of her favorites. Unless they heard anything from the killer, all they had to do today was clean up the petals and candles and enjoy each other's company, and she had a pretty good idea how they would do that.

"Peanut butter," Fletcher replied as he came up behind her, caging her in as he put an arm on either side of her, his hands planted on the countertop as he nuzzled her neck. "Although there's something I'd much rather eat than toast."

He put a hand between her legs, stroking her through her leggings and her body responded instantly.

Who cared about breakfast when this insanely sexy man wanted her in his bed?

Permanently it seemed.

They hadn't talked about how they were going to make their relationship work. He lived here on the east coast, she lived on the west coast, and was less than a year away from finishing her degree, she couldn't just up and leave that behind. And when she graduated, she had hoped to continue working at the veterans' rehab facility, only as a physical therapist instead of just a cleaner and volunteer. Could she give that up to move here? She enjoyed working with vets, but she didn't have to, she could always open her own clinic or see if there were any jobs at the local hospital.

Whatever it took, she was willing to do to make this work with Fletcher.

Fletcher had increased the pressure between her legs, and she moaned and pressed back against him. His hands were just phenomenal, and his mouth … wow … what he could do with that was beyond words.

"So, bed it is?" Fletcher asked, wringing a mumbled protest from her lips when he withdrew his hand.

"I guess we don't need to eat." She spun around to face him, and the heat between her legs increased when she saw what he was wearing. A pair of gray sweatpants hanging low on his hips and nothing else. "Why are you wearing that?"

"What?" he asked, clearly amused.

"Don't you know that gray sweatpants are the sexiest thing a man could wear, and coupled with this body …" she groaned then leaned forward and touched a light kiss between his pecs. "You should come with a warning label."

"Oh yeah?" He raised one eyebrow and gave her that sexy, flirty smile that made her knees go weak. "What would it say?"

"Caution, hot guy ahead, you're about to be burned," she replied. "Only the good kind of burned, the one where your whole body turns to goo because the mind-blowing orgasm you just had melted you."

Fletcher laughed, and the sound almost undid her. How did he manage to get even sexier when he laughed?

"Well, let's go get you your …" Fletcher trailed off as the doorbell rang.

The sound immediately killed her mood. "Is someone coming?" It wasn't that she thought the killer was going to walk right up to Fletcher's front door and try to snatch her straight from his grasp, but she couldn't help the tiny prickle of fear.

"No." From the tense set of his jaw, Dahlia knew he was

worried too. "You wait here."

Although she wanted to stay by his side, felt safer with him next to her, Dahlia did as he asked and waited in the kitchen while he went to the front door. He returned a moment later with a box in his hands.

"Who's that from?" she asked.

"It's addressed to you. You do any online shopping yesterday?"

"No. But it's an Amazon box, and my mom does have a slight addiction to them," she said, attempting to lighten the mood.

Fletcher gave her a half-smile. "Maybe she ordered you something."

He handed her the box, and she grabbed some scissors from the draw and started cutting through the tape. It wasn't until she had it mostly opened that she noticed it. "Fletcher, it looks like this box had tape on it that's already been ripped off," she told him as she noticed the lighter cardboard beneath the tape and the few small tears. "Amazon wouldn't send me something in an old box."

"Stop," Fletcher said, reaching to take the box back, but as he took it the top flaps opened and she got a glimpse at what was inside.

Her knees buckled and she hit the floor hard.

Fletcher cursed and then he was there, scooping her up and carrying her through to the living room where he set her on the sofa and wrapped her in a blanket.

He kissed the top of her head then sat beside her and dragged her onto his lap as he pulled out his phone.

She was glad he'd left the box in the other room, she didn't want to be anywhere near that thing. It wasn't something her mother had ordered for her online, and it wasn't something from Amazon. The killer must have reused a box from something he had previously ordered, then printed off a new label with her name and Fletcher's address.

He knew where she was.

Which meant she wasn't safe here any longer.

And apparently he was no longer content to just send her videos of his crimes he wanted to send her souvenirs too.

Why would he do that?

Why would he send her the three severed fingers he had cut off one of those poor girls' bodies?

Three fingers.

That was the same thing the tuxedo man and his friends had done to Brynn as part of the torture portion of their sick, twisted game.

She didn't understand why he was targeting her.

It had been eight years.

If he was involved in the game back then she didn't know it, she couldn't identify him. She hadn't seen the faces of any of the men who kept her imprisoned except the one who had pretended to be the modeling agent, and he had been killed in the warehouse that day. She was no threat to this man. If he wanted to remain free then targeting her wasn't the way to do it.

Did he want to punish her?

All her previous doubts and the guilt she'd felt about her part in what happened to her and her friends came rushing back. Fletcher and her family said that it wasn't her fault, but maybe this man thought otherwise. Maybe it wasn't about eliminating her as a threat but punishing her for wrong doing.

"It's going to be okay, sweetheart." Lips pressed to her temple in a soft kiss, then Fletcher began to rub her arms, and she realized she was shaking. "Don't let him mess with your head, it's what he wants. We will get him, and he will pay for what he did to those girls and for what he's doing to you."

Fletcher was right, this guy was trying to mess with her head, she didn't know why, but whatever his reasoning was it wasn't because of her. It was his choice to do this. His choice to target her, his choice to hurt those girls, his choice to put himself in a position where death or prison were his only options.

His choice.

Not hers.

"That's my girl," Fletcher said, obviously reading her body language and the way she relaxed further into his hold. "You got this, Freckles, you're too strong to let him break you. Trust your brother and the FBI to find this guy. Trust me to keep you safe until they do."

"I do trust you," she whispered, pressing closer and trying to infuse his heat into her cold body.

The front door opened, and she heard her brothers' and cousins' voices as they walked through the house into the living room.

Levi headed straight for her. "How you doing, honey?" he asked as he pressed the back of his hand to her forehead and cheeks.

"I'm okay."

He untucked the blanket Fletcher had wrapped her in enough to lift her wrist and check her pulse. "She's in shock, but she'll be okay," Levi said, addressing Fletcher. "You'll feel better soon, sweetie," he said to her, placing a comforting hand on her shoulder. "Just got to wait it out I'm afraid."

"Here's some tea," Julian said, carrying a steaming mug over to her. "There's some honey in it too."

"Thanks," she murmured as she took the cup and curled her freezing fingers around it.

"We brought you candy," Will said, holding up her favorite candy bar.

Tears pricked the backs of her eyes, this was so nice, seeing her big tough brothers and cousins fussing over her. Sometimes when she'd been young, she'd hated the age gap because it meant that she wasn't as close to them as they all were with each other. But this made up for it. Having them all here made her feel so much safer, and she knew that the killer would have to get through all of them if he wanted her.

If she had to though she would trade it all for the man who cradled her so gently on his lap. Fletcher was everything she hadn't allowed herself to want but deep down inside hoped for. There was no way she was letting some depraved killer steal her chance at having her dreams come true.

* * * * *

2:16 P.M.

He felt better now that he had Dahlia away from his house. Fletcher had always known that the killer would know when she came back into town, maybe even figure out where she was staying, especially if he was a local. However, knowing that the killer might know where Dahlia was staying and having the killer send severed fingers to the house to torment her were two completely different things.

They couldn't go back to his house until this guy was caught, he hadn't decided yet whether they would stay at one of Dahlia's relative's houses or here at the station, it wouldn't be as comfortable as staying with one of her family, but it would be safer because they wouldn't be endangering anyone else.

For now though they were here, Dahlia was in Abe's office with her mom, Meadow, Maggie, Renee, Mia, and Poppy, while he and the others were gathered in the conference room trying to put together the little they knew about this guy so they could identify him. The FBI had come for the box and would take it away and have their forensic people go over it. Once they had come and gone, he had taken Dahlia upstairs, put her in the shower, and made love to her with the hot water raining down on them, then he'd helped her get dressed, pack her suitcase, and one for himself, then driven her down here.

It meant a lot to both him and Dahlia that her family was rallying around her, supporting her, and trying to help take her mind off things, and while he wasn't surprised he knew Dahlia was. She knew her family loved her, but she was used to pushing them away, and he guessed she thought that she'd pushed too far and for too long and maybe they wouldn't try anymore, having them there for her went a long way toward helping her heal.

"Syd and I have been working on trying to identify possible owners of the van," Beau was saying. "We started with properties closest to the body dump site and are working our way out from there. So far we have a dozen possibilities to look into more closely."

"I know we're looking at the idea that this guy is someone who lives in town, but what are our reasons for thinking that besides the fact that he lured Dahlia back here?" Will asked.

"We were mostly basing that idea on that one fact. Dahlia lives in San Diego and has for the last five years, it would make more sense to target her there, especially since she's more isolated over there, she wouldn't have had the support of family and friends," Julian said.

"So, bringing her back here had to be for a specific reason because it definitely wasn't the smartest idea. Maybe he has ties here, something preventing him from just picking up and leaving," Beau suggested.

"If this guy is from River's End, and from the details he knows about the case and the game, he had to have been involved in the original game, then maybe he was the reason she was abducted in the first place," Sydney suggested.

Everyone looked at her.

When Dahlia and her friends had gone missing the cops had gone through all three of their lives with a fine-tooth comb looking for anyone who might want to hurt them but had come up empty. When someone from the FBI's crimes against children unit happened upon the girls' photos in an online voting game that would rape, torture, and murder teenage girls for money, the idea that either Dahlia or her friends had been specifically targeted had been laid to rest, as it had been assumed they were just an easy mark for the gang. The gang had targeted kids from multiple states, some were runaways, others—like Dahlia—had been lured in under the ruse of a modeling agency.

What if the FBI had been wrong?

Was it possible someone had targeted Dahlia?

"The cops didn't find anything when she was kidnapped," Abe said. None of them had been with the River's End sheriff's department then, but Dahlia's father had been the sheriff, and they knew without a doubt that every man on his team would have looked under every rock to get a lead on who had abducted Dahlia and her friends.

"What if that's because they were looking in the wrong place?" Sydney asked.

"You have an idea?" Fletcher asked her. At this point, he was willing to look into anything, no matter how unlikely because he wanted Dahlia to finally be free.

"Maybe," Sydney said with a nod. "I was looking through all the paperwork on file from the day of the raid. They were able to track the men's credit card information and find out that they were staying at a nearby hotel. When the cops checked the rooms, they found the men's suitcases and belongings, but there were also some comics found under one of the beds. Now I'm not saying that grown men can't read comics, of course they can, but what if we're looking at someone younger. Someone who the cops wouldn't have initially thought could have been involved in Dahlia's kidnapping."

"How young are you thinking?" Abe asked.

"Someone who would have been around the same age as Dahlia when she was fifteen," Sydney replied. "The cops looked for anyone on the sexual offender's register who lived in town. They looked at some people who might have had a beef with your dad and targeted Dahlia to get to him. They looked through some possible suspects who might have targeted Alicia or Brynn, but that was it. No one thought to look at a kid. Now I'm not saying I'm right, I'm just saying that it's a possibility. I know a slim one, chances are those comics did belong to one of the guys, but what if they didn't?"

"What role would a kid have played in this game?" Will asked, looking skeptical.

"Computers," Fletcher said immediately. "If it was someone who wasn't at the warehouse then it had to be the computer guy."

"Were there any boys who Dahlia had problems with?" Beau asked.

Abe shrugged. "We were all away serving when she was in high school so none of us would know, but any boy who asked her out knew that he risked incurring Dahlia's big brothers' wrath if they hurt her." He gave a small chuckle.

"Dahlia used to hate it, a lot of boys wouldn't ask her out because they were kind of scared of us," Theo said, indicating himself, his brothers, cousins, and Fletcher.

"We definitely overdid the whole protective thing, but she was the baby of the family, and none of us wanted to see her hurt," Julian said.

"We can ask Dahlia if there is anyone who stands out," Fletcher said. He wasn't sure how a kid from River's End would connect with a group of men exploiting kids for money, but stranger things had happened.

"Let's go through a list of anyone who was at the high school the same time Dahlia was and find out who still lives in town. Since we think this potential extra person was the gang's computer guy, let's focus on any kid who showed a particular interest or aptitude for coding or hacking or anything else computer related. Let's also start contacting anyone who owns a van and see if they would be willing to let us check it out, blood or recently cleaned puts it on our shortlist along with anyone who says no," Abe gave out the orders.

They didn't have a lot to go on, their best chance at finding this guy was if the forensics team was able to get anything from either the box the killer had sent the fingers in, or one of the bodies, but sometimes you just had to rely on old fashioned police work. Running down any lead no matter how small, making lists and checking people off once you eliminated them as a suspect, interviewing people, and getting a read on their body language and facial expressions. It could be slow, oftentimes tedious work, but it could lead to results just as forensics could.

If Dahlia had been specifically targeted by someone with a grudge against her, the danger she was in increased. It was one thing for someone who thought she might be able to identify him to eliminate a threat, it was another for someone who hated her to want to get their hands on her again. That kind of person would want to make her suffer before he killed her.

Dahlia had already been through enough, more than anyone should have to, and she was just starting to find a way out of the darkness that had enveloped her for so many years. It wasn't fair to see her getting sucked back down into that cold, hard place. But the bustle of his colleagues as they all went to work reassured him. Dahlia didn't just have him to watch her back. She had an entire extended family full of people who would do anything to make sure she was safe.

He'd like to see the killer get through all of them to get to Dahlia.

NOVEMBER 8TH

6:10 A.M.

Nervousness had him twitching, the stakes were so high, one mistake could cost him everything.

This might not be the smartest plan he'd ever had, but Timothy needed to know that Dahlia was dead before he finally left for his new life. Not just because she was a threat to his safety as the only person to have ever survived the RTK game, but also because he just wanted to see her destroyed. He wanted her to know that she wasn't perfect and her life wasn't perfect, that having a family who loved her wasn't going to save her.

There was also the added bonus of knowing that destroying Dahlia would destroy the Black family.

If they thought they were too good for him, too good to bring him into the fold like they had so many other kids in town, then they deserved everything they got.

The three new girls he had grabbed last night were safely tucked away in their cages, and it was time to make his final play. The girls were homeless teens living on the streets of Manhattan. He'd driven out there yesterday after dumping the bodies, waited until dark, then managed to lure in three with some food and a promise of a better life.

Too bad for them there was no better life in their future.

There was no life at all.

All these girls would do was sit in their cells and star in the final video he needed to send Dahlia.

The van had to be returned before he made the video. If he

didn't get rid of it soon there was a chance that someone would be able to link it to him. He didn't think they would, it was a tenuous connection after all, but sometimes cops managed to see things that most people didn't, and the last thing he needed when he was this close to completing his goals was for some cop to have a lightbulb moment.

Content that the girls were safe in his secret location that so far nobody had stumbled upon, he drove the van back through the quiet streets of town. He knew that Dahlia would have received his little gift by now, he'd gone past Fletcher Harris' house on his way back to his land this morning after driving through the night, so he didn't have to waste a day, and when he'd passed it, he'd noted no lights on and no car in the driveway. Fletcher had taken Dahlia and hidden her away someplace, no doubt thinking that would keep her safe when he made a play for the redhead, but he wasn't going to be making a play for her.

He wouldn't have to.

He didn't need to go after Dahlia because she was going to come to him.

By now they had seen him rape, torture, and kill, they knew that he was serious, that he wasn't just playing games, that he was prepared to back up his words with action, so when he told them that the only way to save the lives of the three girls was for Dahlia to offer herself up as the sacrificial lamb she would do it.

Of course, it wasn't true, he couldn't let the girls live, they had seen his face so they had to die, but Dahlia would do it just on the slimmest of chances that those girls could be saved.

Reaching the garage, Timothy unlocked the doors and then drove the van back inside. It would have to be properly cleaned out so there were no traces of blood left in there, but with him running things ever since his father's stroke he was confident that no one would start working on the van until he gave the word. He'd already fixed the vehicle of course, when its owner had dropped it off, he had known that it was the perfect way to transport the girls, so he'd worked on it at night after everyone else had gone home, then borrowed it. What its owner didn't know wouldn't hurt him.

Now the van had become a liability. It was too risky to keep driving it knowing that he might have been spotted yesterday when he dumped the bodies. For now, he would have to go back to using his own truck, and when it was time to dispose of the next lot of bodies, he could figure out what he was going to use to transport them.

Timothy made it back to the shed in good time, and before he went inside, he took a moment to stop and take in the scenery. As soon as he killed Dahlia, he was leaving the country, he already had his ticket bought and paid for and a hotel booked, he was moving to the Maldives where he would be staying in a luxury hotel for the foreseeable future. As far as he was concerned, with the amount of money he had at his disposal he may as well stay in a suite at a hotel where someone would clean for him, and he could order room service for every meal. Maldives had no extradition treaty with the US so once he landed there he was safe. He could live out the rest of his days in paradise.

Never again would he have to live through another snowy winter, but he would miss fall, he loved watching the leaves change color, and Thanksgiving had been one of the few times in the year where his mother would actually come home and stay for a few days, maybe a week or two. Those memories of sitting around the table, turkey, and mashed potatoes, and yams, more food than three people could ever hope to eat, were some of the few good ones he had from his childhood.

Still, he could always have his own Thanksgiving dinner safe in his hotel surrounded by sunshine, blue skies, and sparkling ocean. With his father close to death, and his mother already planning a wedding to the man she had started dating almost as soon as her so-called husband had suffered the stroke that left him all but a vegetable, it wasn't like there was any family to celebrate with here anyway.

This was it. Once he sent that video things would move quickly. He should have Dahlia here and dead by the end of the day, then he would slip his father the drugs that would have him passing peacefully away tomorrow—a more merciful death than the man who had enjoyed hitting him and locking him in a closet when he was a boy deserved—and then the day after that he would be driving to the airport and getting on that plane. Anything he couldn't live without was going in that suitcase with him, everything else would be left behind.

Peace settled on him now, washing away the tension and nerves. He'd come this far he could finish this off. The worst was behind him. The three girls he had in there would be eliminated with a simple bullet between the eyes and he was determined not to mess that up again. He wasn't quite sure what he had planned for Dahlia, but it wouldn't be that simple or that quick and painless.

Heading inside the shed, he looked at the three girls curled up in the corners of their cells. There was nothing he could say to reassure him, they weren't stupid, they knew they were in trouble, that they wouldn't be walking out of here alive, so he ignored them and went to the camera, pulling on his mask before turning it on.

Then he stepped back and allowed the lens to take in the three girls. Dahlia needed to see them and know that these were the people who would die in her place if she didn't agree to his terms. Once she had seen them she wouldn't be able to do anything but come and meet with him.

Stepping in front of the camera, he gave the short speech he had prepared. "You know what I did to the other three girls. The RTK game can end but only if you're prepared to offer yourself in exchange for these girls. If you don't, then you know what their fate will be, and I won't stop there. It's up to you, Dahlia, only you can save them. Either you meet me in an hour at the address I'm going to include in the message with this video, or I start the game. Rape, torture, kill, which girl will meet which fate?"

Timothy crossed to the camera and switched it off. He'd laid the trap, and now the only thing he could do was wait to see if Dahlia was going to step up and follow his instructions or whether she needed further motivation. He hoped it was the former because he really didn't want to have to reschedule his flight. He was ready to start his new life in paradise.

* * * * *

8:58 A.M.

Dahlia drank her coffee and openly stared at Fletcher as he stood talking to Abe. He looked so sexy in his jeans and sweater, his hands were curled around a mug of coffee, and she found herself fixated on those fingers. She loved the feel of them stroking deep inside her, and she loved the feel of them tracing across her skin, and she loved the feel of them curled around her own fingers …

"Dahlia."

She blinked and looked up to find Fletcher watching her with an amused expression, it was clear he was saying something to her, but she'd been too busy daydreaming about him touching her. Ignoring the burning in her cheeks, she focused on him. "Sorry, I was thinking about something."

Fletcher leaned in close to whisper in her ear. "I'd love to know what you were thinking about, but I think I can make a pretty good guess, and as soon as I get you back to my place I'm not letting you out of my bed for a week."

Heat pooled between her legs, and she shifted uncomfortably wishing they could go back to Fletcher's right now. They'd stayed here at the station last night with Abe and her cousins taking shifts staying here with them just in case the killer made an attempt to snatch her, and they'd be staying here until they had him in custody, but she couldn't wait to be alone with Fletcher again. "I'm going to hold you to that."

He kissed her cheek then straightened. "So, Abe and I were discussing …"

Fletcher trailed off when they heard her phone ring.

The killer.

It had to be him sending her another video.

He'd killed the first three girls. Had he taken more?

Abe picked up her phone, and Dahlia curled her hand around Fletcher's, clinging to him and drawing in his strength as they waited to see what the killer had to tell them.

A moment later, a voice filled the conference room that had gone otherwise silent.

"You know what I did to the other three girls. The RTK game can end but only if you're prepared to offer yourself in exchange for these girls. If you don't, then you know what their fate will be, and I won't stop there. It's up to you, Dahlia, only you can save them. Either you meet me in an hour at the address I'm going to include in the message with this video, or I start the game. Rape, torture, kill, which girl will meet which fate?"

No one spoke right away when the voice stopped talking.

All she could think of was getting to that address as quickly as she could.

She had to.

How could she let three more girls go through what she and her friends had?

She couldn't.

She had to go.

"Dahlia, do you recognize the voice?" Abe asked.

"What? No." She didn't care about who it was, she just wanted to hurry up and get to whatever address he'd included in the text. Dropping Fletcher's hand, she launched to her feet, scanning the room for his keys. "We have to go. He said I only have an hour to be there. Where are we going?"

Abe, Fletcher, Will, Julian, Sydney, and Beau exchanged glances. "Sweetheart, you're not going to meet him," Fletcher said gently.

"I have to. You heard what he said, he's going to play the game with them if I don't show up." As she said the words, she was already figuring out if she could get out of here if they decided they didn't want her to go. If she knew her brother and cousins they would handcuff her and throw her in a cell before they would let her go.

"Sweetheart, it's a trap," Fletcher said, grasping her shoulders and making her look at him.

"I know, but what choice do we have?" she demanded. She wasn't stupid, she knew that as soon as she turned up at this guy's chosen location, he was likely to kill her. "I don't have to go alone, we can set a trap of our own. You guys can follow me or get there first, and then you can get him, and we can save those girls."

"Sit down, Dahlia," Abe said, his I'm your older brother and therefore the boss of you voice firmly in place. She did only because she wanted to get things moving as soon as possible. "We are going to set a trap for him, but you're not going to be part of it. Even if you weren't my little sister, there would be no way I'd risk your safety, and if you think I'm going to let you get anywhere near this guy and risk having to face mom and dad and tell them that I got you hurt or killed then you don't know me very well. You and Sydney are close enough in height and size that I think she could pass for you if we put her in your clothes and give her a red wig. Fletcher will take you someplace safe while this guy is distracted, the rest of us will follow Sydney to the meeting point. We'll get him," Abe promised.

Dahlia chewed on her bottom lip. This plan could work if this guy believed that Sydney was her long enough for her to get close to him. If he didn't then not only those three girls could die, but her soon-to-be sister-in-law as well. On the other hand, the idea of going anywhere near someone who had been involved in her abduction and rape made her feel sick.

"What if he doesn't believe that she's me?" Dahlia asked. No way did she want to have to look her brother Levi in the eye ever again if his fiancée got killed because of her. Levi had already lost two women he loved, and Dahlia didn't think he could survive losing a third.

"We know what we're doing, Dahlia," Abe assured her. "We'll have the area surrounded, he'll never know we're there. And Sydney knows what she's doing. Bottom line is, I won't put you in danger and I think this will work."

"I'm happy to do it," Sydney reassured her.

"Everything will work out okay," Fletcher promised.

Since it seemed like she didn't have a choice in the matter, Dahlia nodded her agreement. Abe, Will, and Julian had all served in the military before becoming cops, and Beau and Sydney had both been cops for several years, they were all well trained, and she had to trust that they could catch this guy, beat him at his own game.

Abe squeezed her hand before he started giving orders. "Will, Julian, and Beau, you guys head out now, it will take you at least twenty minutes to get to the meeting point, and I want you there before him so you can be in position. I'll follow Sydney, so let's get her dressed in some of Dahlia's clothes, and I'll send Poppy out to find a wig. Fletcher, you take Dahlia now, get her out to Maggie's hotel, he'll be distracted thinking that she's coming to him so he won't know where she is if things don't work and he manages to slip away."

Hating the idea that her brother and cousins were in danger because of her, Dahlia stood and wrapped her arms around Abe's waist. "Be careful, please."

If he was surprised by her display of affection he didn't show it, just held her close. "You know it, little sister."

She hugged Will and Julian as well before going to Sydney and holding her tightly. "Don't get hurt."

"I won't," Sydney promised.

"Come on," Fletcher said, taking her hand and guiding her out of the room.

She didn't want to go, didn't like the idea of her family in danger because of her, but she had to admit that Sydney was a lot more experienced than she was and stood a much better chance at getting the result they all wanted. Dahlia definitely wasn't so stubborn she would insist on putting herself in danger just on principle when the others would be safer without her in the picture.

They didn't talk as Fletcher drove them through town, and they were halfway between the town and the property where the hotel Maggie had inherited from her grandparents sat, when the car suddenly died.

"What happened?" she asked.

"I don't know, no lights came on, the engine just died," Fletcher replied.

"Terrible time for the car to break down," she said.

"Agreed." Fletcher pressed the engine start button again, then pulled out the fob that connected to the car's computer system and pressed it.

Nothing.

"Looks like the car's computer system has died," Fletcher said, "we're going to have to call the mechanic."

It was clear from his tone that he was on edge, wondering if this was a game the killer was playing. Could he know that they were planning on tricking him and sending Sydney to impersonate her instead?

Fletcher called the mechanic, and then there was nothing for the two of them to do but wait. They were both edgy, and they sat in silence, Fletcher holding her hand as they waited for the tow truck.

"Did you tell Abe?" she asked. If this was the killer playing games then she didn't like the idea of everyone else being out on the other side of town and her and Fletcher alone out here. She trusted him implicitly, but that didn't mean that he could protect her against every conceivable threat. He was only human, the bullet wound he'd gotten last time he came riding in to rescue her proved that.

"Sent him a text."

"Good," she murmured before lapsing back into silence.

Another ten minutes passed before she caught sight of the tow truck pulling up behind them.

"Stay in the car," Fletcher told her as he opened his door and climbed out.

Knowing better than to argue, she stayed where she was, twisting in her seat to watch Fletcher as he rounded the car and waited until Timothy Jay climbing out of the tow truck.

A weird feeling prickled in her stomach.

The hint of a memory.

Timothy at school, always hidden behind a computer screen.

Timothy asking her out but her younger self turning him down because she was crushing on Fletcher.

Timothy fiddling with the camera while Dahlia and her friends huddled naked in their cells.

Before she could fit everything together and yell out a warning, a gunshot echoed through the quiet fall day, and Fletcher dropped to the ground.

No.

This couldn't be happening again.

Timothy was the killer, and he'd just shot Fletcher.

* * * * *

10:04 A.M.

Fletcher groaned as he came to.

Pain burned in his chest, but the instinctive feeling that something was wrong tugged him quickly out of unconsciousness, and he surged to his feet.

He was lying on the side of the road, in a puddle of blood. Blood also drenched the front of his sweater. His truck was beside him, both the front driver and passenger doors were open, but it appeared empty.

Dahlia.

The killer had her.

Timothy Jay.

A year older than Dahlia, computer lover, lived in River's End all his life, father ran one of the three local mechanics and had recently suffered a stroke, and from what he'd heard, could pass any day now. Mother was CEO of some big clothing company and hardly ever around. Timothy Jay was the killer. How the then sixteen-year-old had managed to get himself mixed in with the criminal gang that ran the RTK game Fletcher had no idea, but it was obvious that Timothy had been involved, he knew too much.

And now he had Dahlia.

Fletcher reached for his cell in his back pocket, wincing at the tearing in his chest. As he dialed Abe, he sagged against the back of his vehicle, blood loss making him woozy.

He had to pull it together.

Dahlia needed him.

He had promised her he would protect her, keep her safe, assured her that he wouldn't let anyone hurt her ever again.

He had failed.

"He never showed," Abe said without preamble when he answered the phone.

"Didn't have to," he grunted.

Immediately alert, Abe's voice tensed. "What happened?"

"Trap. Somehow he managed to get control of the car's computer system, shut it down, I called for a tow truck. He shot me." Fletcher was almost out of breath by the time he relayed that to Abe.

"Shot you?" Abe repeated. "How bad?"

"I'm not going to die," he replied.

"Dahlia?"

He heard the fear in his boss' voice, hated to break the news that he had failed to keep Abe's baby sister safe. "Gone."

Abe swore. "We're coming to you, and I'll call an ambulance."

"No," he said firmly—no way was he being sidelined now. "Levi can stitch me up. Not going to a hospital while she's out there somewhere with him."

The sheriff made a non-committal noise. "Be there as quickly as we can. Don't bleed out before we do."

"Don't plan on it."

Once he hung up the phone, Fletcher propped himself up against the truck. He had to hold on, had to find a way to pull it together. When they found her, Dahlia would need him, and no way was he not going to be there for her this time. She'd shut him out last time, he got it she'd been a traumatized fifteen-year-old who blamed herself for a lot of things including him getting shot, but this time he was going to be the one to hold her, comfort her, reassure her.

She was his.

Despite his best efforts to remain awake, his eyes slid closed, and it wasn't until he heard car doors slamming and footsteps approaching that he jerked awake. When he saw his team approaching, he tried to get to his feet, but Levi dropped down beside him and held a hand to his shoulder.

"Don't get up, let me see how bad this is," Levi said.

Fletcher grunted when the doctor pulled his sweater away from the bullet wound. Hurt like hell, but he was awake, he could think and move, as far as he was concerned he was good to go as soon as Levi stitched him up.

"Lean forward so I can see if there's an exit wound," Levi said then carefully helped him ease away from the vehicle, probably the only thing preventing him from keeling over. "Through and through," Levi said. "I can stitch you up but given the amount of blood you lost." The doctor paused to turn and look at the large puddle of blood on the ground. "You need to go to the hospital."

"Not happening. Dahlia is out there."

"And we'll find her," Abe said, crouching on Fletcher's other side.

"Not sitting this out," he gritted out through clenched teeth. He needed all his energy to focus on finding Dahlia not on arguing with his boss.

"Look, I know you two are a couple, I get that you care about her, but she's our sister," Abe said, gesturing between himself Levi and Theo who stood off to the side, arms crossed over his chest, a scowl on his face. "She's Will and Julian's cousin. Sydney's soon-to-be sister-in-law, you really think we aren't going to do everything we can to find her, bring her home?"

"Doesn't matter. I have to be there." Fletcher couldn't explain it; it was as simple as that. Dahlia needed him, had trusted him, he wouldn't—couldn't—not be there when they found her.

Abe sighed but stopped arguing. "Put him in the back of my car and stitch him up," he said to Levi, who helped him up, steadied him when he swayed, then guided him to Abe's car. "You see who shot you?"

"Timothy Jay," he replied, focusing on Abe rather than on what Levi was doing to his chest. The bullet had hit him in virtually the same place it had last time, thankfully missing his shoulder joint, his heart, his lung, or any arteries. He'd be sore as heck, weak from blood loss, but he was functional.

"Timothy?" Abe's eyes went round, and the faces of the others—who had gathered around the open car door—looked equally as shocked.

"You sure?" Will asked.

"Positive. I saw him drive up and had my hand on my weapon

because I knew it could be a trap, but he didn't hesitate and shot me as he was climbing out of the car. Must have grabbed Dahlia, I don't know if he shot her too, but given that she isn't sitting dead in the car I'm guessing he didn't." The thought of her being gone left him feeling hollow. She meant a lot to him, he cared about her more than he'd ever cared about another human being, and he couldn't even allow himself to wonder what she was going through right this second because if he did he was going to lose it.

"Yeah, he wants her alive," Julian agreed. "Wants her to suffer."

"Chances are he took her wherever he has the other girls," Sydney said. "He'll want her to watch him kill them, make sure she knows he's doing it because of her."

"Dahlia is stronger than you all give her credit for, she'll fight him, she's not going to just stand there and let him kill her," Beau said, making sure to look each of them in the eye.

Beau was right. She was strong, and there was no way she was going to go down without a fight. She had a lot to live for, and he was honored to know that he was a large part of that.

"We have to find where Timothy is holed up," Fletcher said, trying not to wince as the needle pulled through his torn flesh as Levi put in another stitch.

"On it," Sydney said, pulling out her phone and tapping away. "I'm going to get us a warrant to look into his financials, one for the business too. If he wanted to stay under the radar he could have bought or rented a piece of land under the business name."

"Could have driven a van that was at the garage too," Will suggested. "We should check out any in the shop and see if there's blood in them that matches the three girls."

"It can't be too far out of town," Julian said thoughtfully. "And we know which direction he was driving when he dumped the bodies because we have a witness. Assuming he came straight from wherever he's hiding out then we know what side of town to focus our search."

"Can't be too far out of town, he has to be able to get there quickly. He's caring for his dying father as well as running the garage," Will added.

"And has to be secluded enough that no one will hear the girls scream or the sound of gunshots," Beau said.

"He hasn't been planning this too long, not more than a couple of months, probably since his father's stroke back in July. It would be quicker to search for any properties recently sold or rented than to wait for the warrants for Timothy's financials," Abe said. "Let's find where he's holed himself up and go find our girl."

Fletcher couldn't agree more. As Levi taped a bandage over the entry wound and helped him turn around so he could work on the exit wound Fletcher focused on Dahlia. *We're coming, Freckles.* I'm *coming. You just hold on, do whatever you have to to stay alive until we get there.*

* * * * *

10:30 A.M.

Pain splintered her skull into a thousand pieces.

Darkness crashed at her, threatening to pull her right back under as soon as she started to surface, but some distant warning prickled at her already aching head, so she clung to the consciousness that was only just returning.

Dahlia forced herself to focus. Whatever was going on here was too important for her to blank out, she had to get it together.

She cracked her eyes open and found herself sprawled on the backseat of a car. She wasn't buckled in, one leg was wedged between the passenger seat and the backseat. Despite the pain in her head, she didn't think she was hurt anywhere else. There was only one other person in the car, and he was the one driving.

The vehicle turned a corner, and she groaned in pain as she

slid sideways, the pain in her head so bad she couldn't think of anything else.

The darkness was back, tugging at her with a soft touch urging her to give into it and enjoy the peace it offered, but she fought against it.

She had to stay awake.

She knew that, even as she didn't know why or what danger she was in.

The vehicle turned again, and the tires must have rolled over something because she heard a crack, and immediately a barrage of memories assaulted her, each one like another knife being stuck into her already throbbing head.

She remembered the crack of a gunshot and Fletcher going down.

Was he dead?

Her heart rate accelerated at the thought. How would she live with herself if he had died because someone was after her?

No.

Not someone.

Timothy.

Timothy Jay.

She didn't know why, but he wanted her dead.

And he might have killed the man she loved to make it happen.

The idea that she loved Fletcher didn't come as a shock to her, she'd always loved him. Over time that love had grown from teenage puppy love to something stronger, firmer, almost overwhelming. His unwavering support, his gentle touch, his calm words, they'd all cracked away at the barrier she had built around herself to protect her battered soul. Now he was through, all the way in, and she was glad.

Fiery determination sparked inside her.

If Timothy had killed Fletcher, then she would destroy him, and if Fletcher had survived the gunshot, then she would do whatever it took to get back to him.

The car stopped moving, and Dahlia weighed her options. Last time she'd been kidnapped she'd been helpless, just a girl, drugged, and waking already imprisoned and without options to save herself.

This time that wasn't happening.

No way would she allow him to lock her up or tie her up.

She was fighting with everything that she had.

She was the baby of her family with a former military father, three former military big brothers, and two former military older cousins, she knew more self-defense moves than any other person could possibly know. Okay, she had a concussion because Timothy had slammed his gun into her head when she fought him as he tried to abduct her, that meant she was at a disadvantage, but she wasn't giving up.

She couldn't.

If she was going to die at Timothy's hand, she wouldn't make it easy for him.

Just a week ago if he'd come for her she probably would have just given up, let him kill her, she hadn't had anything to live for then.

But she did now.

Somehow Fletcher had managed to give her her life back as well as her confidence, and she wanted more than anything a chance to see if he could fall in love with her too.

The door behind her head was wrenched open, and she was grabbed roughly under the arms and dragged out. The movement had a vicious pain twisting in her head, and her stomach revolted, filling her with sickening nausea.

Timothy flung her over his shoulder, and her trembling limbs could do nothing but hang limply and uselessly.

They were in a small clearing, and Timothy was walking her toward a large shed. That had to be where he had the three girls he'd kidnapped to try to lure her out here. A plan began to form in her fuzzy mind. Whether Fletcher was dead or not the others had to know that Timothy hadn't shown up at the location he'd set up to try to get to her. They'd know that something was wrong, and when they found Fletcher shot, they'd know that Timothy had her. It didn't matter if they knew Timothy's identity or not, they'd know she was gone and they'd be looking for her. Dahlia had every faith in them to find her which meant all she had to do was stay alive until they got here. Once she confirmed that the girls were there, all she had to do was get away and make a run for the trees. She was what Timothy wanted, he'd leave the girls to chase after her so she'd have to avoid him long enough to give the others time.

She could do that.

Wasn't like she had a choice, she *had* to do that.

Each step Timothy took sent a fresh wave of pain through her head, but she did her best to shove it away. She breathed through her nose, tried to focus, prepared her body for what she knew wasn't going to be an easy fight.

"I've waited a long time to do this," Timothy said as he reached the shed, pausing to unlock the door.

"Why?" she croaked.

"Because you had everything," he roared, the loud sound sending arrows of pain shooting inside her skull.

"Everything?"

"A family who adored you, father who was the sheriff, mother who took in all the town stray's, all except me," he sneered. "Your family thought it was so perfect, the heart of the town, everyone loved you, and you didn't even realize what you had. I took you down and your family with you."

"You told the gang about me," she said as she realized what he was saying. Timothy had sold her out, not just participated in the game but actively set out to see her murdered or sold because those would have been her only two paths once the game was played.

"You weren't supposed to survive, and I would have been free with more money than I could ever have known what to do with. I waited, knew eventually I would get you, and now it's time, my father is dying and I'll finally be free of him. But if I want to truly live in peace you have to die. It's win, win, win. You'll be dead, your family will be destroyed, and I can get out of River's End and do whatever I want with my life."

Timothy opened the door and swung sideways to step through with her on his shoulder. The movement sent her stomach lurching, and as she caught sight of the three girls huddled in cages, Dahlia didn't fight it when bile burned in her throat. She threw up down Timothy's back, making him curse and drop her. She hit the concrete ground hard and lay there stunned for a moment.

"That's disgusting," he growled.

With Timothy distracted, Dahlia took the only opportunity she would get to escape. Staggering to her feet she ran.

"You won't get away," Timothy yelled after her, and he shot at her.

Dahlia knew to run in a zigzag pattern to make herself a harder target to hit, and the bullet whizzed past her.

She slowed when she reached the tree line, needing to catch her breath and quell the dizziness that had the world spinning around her. She could hear Timothy running toward her, and knowing she couldn't outrun him with a concussion, she scanned the area, her gaze landing on a large stick.

Scooping it up, she curled her shaking hands around it and prayed she had enough strength to stun him enough that she could get away, or if she was really lucky, get custody of the gun.

Leaning against a tree for support, the second Timothy came rushing past, Dahlia swung with everything she had, hitting Timothy on the back of the head and making him fall to his knees.

The gun fell from his grip, and Dahlia awkwardly stumbled

toward it. If she could just get to it she'd kill Timothy. The idea of taking a life should leave her conflicted, but it didn't, this man had been responsible for what happened to her, and he'd done it to destroy her family. Her family might not be perfect, but they loved wholly and completely. They didn't deserve what Timothy had tried to do to them.

Just as her fingers brushed the cool metal of the gun, Timothy knocked into her from behind, sending her sprawling onto her stomach.

"You're not getting away from me, I want to be free," Timothy roared as he grabbed the gun.

Dahlia slammed her head back, crying out in pain when it connected with Timothy's chin, but she was able to dislodge him enough that she could turn around onto her back and slam the wood that she still held into his groin.

Timothy howled when it connected and dropped sideways allowing her to scramble to her feet and start running again.

Well, she wasn't so much running as she was lurching unsteadily through the forest. Branches snagged on her hair as she ran and she yanked it free without stopping, sharp stings on her face told her that those same branches were scratching at her exposed skin, but she didn't have time to worry about that.

She had no idea how long she ran, all she knew was that her lungs heaved trying to get enough oxygen, her head was fuzzy, her vision blurry, and she had no idea which direction she was running in. At this point it was pure adrenaline and determination keeping her on her feet, but she knew that it couldn't keep her going indefinitely.

Dahlia reached the river and was just debating whether she should stop, try to figure out where she was, and where she could hide herself away when she was tackled from behind. She and Timothy both plunged into the icy river, the cold stealing her breath.

Timothy flipped her onto her back, his hands gripped her

shoulders as he straddled her, gripping her hips between his knees, keeping her immobile and completely at his mercy.

"You're not getting away from me," Timothy said again, his eyes wild as he stared down at her. "Your family will pay for thinking they're too good to bring me into the fold by losing their precious little princess. You are going to die and then I will be free."

With that, he shoved her head under the water and held it there.

This was it.

The end.

She'd done the best she could, but it hadn't been enough.

Timothy was going to kill her.

Dahlia held her breath for as long as she could, she kicked and tried to dislodge Timothy's hands, but in the end, the result was inevitable.

Before death claimed her, Dahlia sent one last thought into the universe and hoped that somehow, someway, it made it to Fletcher. *Thank you for believing in me, for helping me, I love you.*

* * * * *

11:11 A.M.

"We've narrowed it down to two properties that are most likely ones Timothy is using," Sydney announced from the backseat.

Fletcher would have turned to face her, but that would hurt too much so instead he merely asked, "Which two?"

"The old Hatfield farm, and the Reiners decided to get rid of some of their property because it got too big to handle," Sydney replied.

"Rented or sold?" Abe asked from the driver's seat.

"Hatfield farm was sold, and the Reiners' rented the land so they would have extra income," Sydney answered. "Both went through about six months ago, within weeks of Timothy's father's stroke, so they definitely fit the timeline. We won't have access to Timothy's financials until we get the warrant, which shouldn't be long."

But possibly longer than Dahlia had.

The more time she was in Timothy's clutches, the less the chances that they would get her back alive.

She'd already been with him long enough for him to have hurt her.

"Reiners' land," Fletcher said, going with his gut.

"Why do you think that?" Levi asked from the backseat where he sat next to Sydney. Will, Julian, Theo, and Beau were following in another vehicle. Everyone was in on this because they knew how dangerous Timothy was.

"He's going to want to bail as soon as he has what he wants which is Dahlia dead. It's easier to break a lease than it is to have to organize the sale of land you no longer want," Fletcher said. He had learned as a kid to trust his gut when it came to the men his mom brought in and out of his and Florence's lives. That skill had been honed in his years serving in the military, and in his years as a cop. If his gut said the Reiners' property, then that's where they were going.

"Makes sense," Abe said, taking the next right which would lead them out to the property in question. "When we get there you're staying in the car with Levi."

"No," Fletcher said simply. Dahlia was his, and he was going to be the one to save her.

"Yes," Abe countered calmly.

"I'm not a liability," he said. "I can do this. I *have* to do this. I promised her that I wouldn't let this guy get her and I failed. I'm going to be there for her. No way I'm sitting in the car while you guys go after her."

Abe sighed but didn't say anything else, and the rest of the drive passed in silence. Fifteen minutes later they were pulling up outside the Reiners' remote property.

"Mr. Reiner says to keep going for another mile then there's a dirt road leading to the part of the property they rented out," Sydney said from the phone where she'd obviously managed to get in contact with the couple.

Abe followed her instructions, and soon they were turning down the barely visible dirt road. It was taking too long. He wanted to be on the ground searching for Dahlia, taking Timothy down, ending this so Dahlia would be free.

"Building up ahead," Abe said quietly, and Sydney relayed that to the other car, having changed calls and switched to the guys. "FBI is on the way, they want Timothy alive because they want to find out if there is anyone else left from the game. Personally, I don't care one way or the other our priority is Dahlia and the other girls. If we can take Timothy alive we will, but if he's a threat to Dahlia and won't cooperate then we take him out."

As they all climbed out of the cars, Fletcher knew the others wanted the same thing that he did.

Timothy Jay dead.

That was the only way Dahlia was ever going to truly feel free.

Ignoring the pain in his chest which had dulled to a distant ache, wildly overshadowed by the pain in his heart knowing Dahlia needed him and he wasn't there for her, he lifted his weapon, and they all moved in on the building.

It looked like one of those shed kits that you could assemble yourself, maybe about twenty feet by twenty feet, and Fletcher had to wonder how Timothy had gotten the building erected on his own. It was definitely remote out here, no one would hear the girls' screams or the gunshots, and he was free to move the bodies without fear of anyone noticing.

The first thing he noticed as they reached the metal building was the smell. Blood, sweat, human waste, and something stronger. Vomit. Fresh vomit.

Abe went in first, the rest of them following behind, and found only three terrified young girls in cages across the far wall.

No sign of Dahlia.

"It's okay, we're the police," Sydney said, holstering her weapon and moving cautiously toward the traumatized girls. "Do you know where the man is who took you?"

"H-he ran," one of the girls said, inching closer. "He brought another woman here. He was carrying her over his shoulder, she threw up, and she ran when he put her down. He went after her."

"Was she hurt?" he demanded, more forcefully than he should, and the girls flinched at his tone.

"She had blood on her head," the girl replied.

"Concussion," Levi said, nodding to the vomit. "She probably knew that if she threw up on him he'd be distracted, let her go long enough that she could get away."

His brave girl was amazing. She was clearly injured, and yet she had to know they would be coming for her and that all she had to do was stay alive until they got there. She'd also known that she was the real target and that Timothy would go after her, meaning she also kept these three girls safe.

"They're going to be more comfortable with a woman right now," Abe said, gesturing at the three girls, "so, Sydney, you stay here with them, Beau too, get them out and call-in ambulances. Levi, you can stay and look them over."

"No," Levi said forcefully. "Dahlia is hurt, I'm going with you. She's going to need me when we find her. I may not be a cop, but I know what I'm doing, I won't be in the way. The girls look okay, Sydney and Beau can get them blankets and water and wait for the paramedics to show up."

"Can we just get going," Fletcher said, getting antsier by the second. Dahlia was out there being hunted by a psychopath, and while she'd done amazingly well on her own and given herself a chance, she was waiting on them to come and find her.

"Yeah, let's go." Abe nodded.

"Be careful," Sydney said to Levi, giving him a quick kiss, then she and Beau stayed behind, and the rest of them headed for the forest.

There was no way to know which direction Dahlia had taken when she'd run. She was hurt and not thinking of anything but getting away so they couldn't predict if she would have headed for a road or the closest property or just run wildly. They split up as they hit the trees, and everything else faded from his mind as he ran, everything except Dahlia. Her pretty face hovered in front of him silently pleading for his help.

He was close to the river when he heard it.

The sounds of splashing.

"Your family will pay for thinking they're too good to bring me into the fold by losing their precious little princess. You are going to die and then I will be free," a voice growled.

Timothy's voice.

He'd found them.

Fletcher picked up the pace and burst out through the trees, his weapon aimed at Timothy who stood in waist-deep water. He couldn't see Dahlia, but Timothy was clearly holding something—some*one*—under the water.

"Let her go, Timothy," he said, his voice quietly menacing. "It's over."

Timothy's head whipped around in surprise. "You're too late," he said with a near manic grin. "She stopped fighting, she's already dead. It's done." The last was said like he was relieved that his goal had been achieved.

Refusing to believe he had arrived too late, Fletcher's aim didn't waver. "Let go of her, get out of the water, and put your hands behind your head." His finger itched to pull the trigger, end this here and now, but the FBI wanted this guy alive, and he would do his best to make sure Timothy stayed that way.

To his surprise, Timothy let go of Dahlia and walked from the river. "It doesn't matter. Dahlia is dead, and the Black family will never recover from the loss."

This guy had a real hard-on for the Black family, but he didn't particularly care about why Timothy hated them, he just wanted the guy cuffed so he could get to Dahlia. "Hands on your head," he ordered.

Timothy nodded but then lifted a weapon and fired. Fletcher reacted at the same time, firing a shot of his own that hit the guy in the shoulder, sending the weapon falling from his grip as he screamed and dropped to his knees.

Fletcher ran forward, grabbing the other gun, then ignoring Timothy who wouldn't get far even if he tried to run, his entire focus on Dahlia who was floating limply in the cold river. He grunted as he scooped Dahlia into his arms, his stitches pulling, then carried her up and laid her down on the bank. Her skin was devoid of color, and he winced as he pressed his fingers to her neck in search of a pulse.

He couldn't find one.

He placed his cheek above her mouth, willing her to be breathing, but he didn't feel a puff of air against his skin or see her chest rise and fall as it drew a breath.

Action exploded around him as the gunshots drew the others, and a moment later he was gently pushed out of the way as Levi dropped down beside him.

"Is she breathing?" Levi demanded even as he touched Dahlia's neck.

"No," he said, the word feeling like it tore through his throat as it came out.

Dahlia wasn't breathing.

She was gone.

Levi didn't hesitate, just pinched his sister's nose, tilted her head back, and breathed into her.

When Fletcher went to start chest compressions Abe nudged him out of the way. "You can't, you'll tear your stitches."

While Dahlia's brothers performed CPR, all Fletcher could do was smooth the wet locks of hair off her face and stroke her cheek, silently pleading with her to come back. He could hear other voices but no more gunshots and knew that Will and Julian had Timothy under control.

"Come on, sweetheart," he begged as Levi and Abe started their third round of CPR. "Don't be gone."

The seconds ticked by with excruciating slowness as each one passed, Dahlia's chances of reviving slipped further away.

"Fletcher, if she doesn't—"

"Don't stop," he ordered, cutting Levi off.

"We're not stopping." Levi looked insulted by the prospect. "But you need to be prepared." He paused as Abe finished chest compressions and breathed two more breaths into Dahlia's still form. "She was already hurt before he got her in the water, she's not responding, the chances that …" he trailed off as the most miraculous sound filled the cold day. Dahlia coughed and spluttered, her waterlogged lungs attempting to suck in air.

"That's it, sweetheart," Fletcher said, continuing to caress her cheek as Levi rolled her over so she could cough up the water that had almost stolen her from him.

When Abe and Levi lowered her back down, her unfocused gaze moved about before settling on one of her brothers. "Levi," she croaked, reaching for him. Levi gathered her into his arms as she sobbed and continued to cough.

"Shh," Levi soothed, holding her tight. "You're going to be okay."

"Fletcher," she asked against her brother's shoulder.

"Is right here," Levi said as he gently passed his precious bundle over into Fletcher's waiting arms.

"I got you, baby, I'm here, I'm okay, you're going to be okay, it's over," he promised as he touched kisses all over her face and then finally pressed his lips to hers.

"I l-l-love you," she said as she clutched at him.

"I love you too, Freckles," he said with a smile and a laugh that turned into a sob and buried his face in her wet hair, holding onto her and knowing he was never going to let her go. She was his, and they would find a way to make it work between them.

"We have to get her out of those wet clothes and back to the ambulance," Levi said, resting one hand on his shoulder, the other was on Dahlia's back as though he couldn't bear to break contact with her. Fletcher knew her family had been as terrified of losing her as he had been. *Almost* as terrified. Because he couldn't imagine anyone loving the shaking woman he held close to his heart more than he did.

"You won't be able to carry her," Abe reminded him.

Letting her go wasn't an option, but Abe was right, there was no way he could carry her through the forest with a bullet hole beneath his shoulder. "Not letting her go," he said, pulling Dahlia tighter into his embrace.

"We're only a few hundred yards from the road if we head south instead of going back to the shed," Theo said, appearing beside him with a blanket. "We can help him make it that far."

Relieved, Fletcher loosened his hold on Dahlia only enough that her brothers could help strip off her soaked clothes, then he wrapped her in the blanket, and with Abe and Levi's help, he got to his feet with Dahlia in his arms. She was shaking so hard her teeth chattered, and he knew she was hurting besides the cold, but she was alive and she was safe. Timothy was also alive and would face the consequences of his choices, giving Dahlia the justice she deserved.

Dahlia would leave the forest surrounded by family, the people who loved her and would forever unwaveringly support her. Never again would she shoulder the blame for things outside her control, never again would she doubt how others saw her, never again would she doubt herself. He would make sure of it.

NOVEMBER 9TH

3:41 P.M.

"I kind of expected the whole army to be here when they finally discharged me," Dahlia said as the nurse pushed her in a wheelchair toward the hospital's exit. "And how come I have to sit in a wheelchair and you get to walk. You were shot." She gave Fletcher a small glare, then frowned as it made her head hurt worse.

"I think that's why you're in the wheelchair," Fletcher replied with a wry smile. "You wince every time you move."

"And you don't?" She'd been in and out of consciousness after she'd been brought to the hospital the day before. She'd been poked and prodded, sent for scans and tests, and treated for a concussion and mild hypothermia. Fletcher had refused to be checked out until she was finally settled in a room and had drifted off to sleep. And only then after she was surrounded by pretty much her entire family. They hardly all fit in the hospital room, but they'd all come to be with her, wanting her to know that she was surrounded by love and support. It had made her cry—still made her teary—to think about, and she was surprised that after making sure some of the Black family was with her through the night, after lunch they all seemed to have disappeared.

"I'm fine, Freckles," Fletcher said, taking her hand and squeezing it.

"You got shot because of me. Again," she corrected, frowning at the spot on his shoulder where she knew there was a bandage taped under his shirt. She winced again as the movement made the lump on her temple and the row of stitches Levi had put in ache.

"Stop doing that," Fletcher reprimanded gently, smoothing a thumb across her forehead.

Dahlia relaxed and reached for his hand again. Once they got outside the hospital, Fletcher reached down and wrapped an arm around her waist, helping her stand and steadying her as she got her balance. Dizziness, headaches, tiredness, Levi had told her it would take a few days at least, maybe longer, for the effects of the concussion to fade, and in addition to that her chest was sore from her brothers performing CPR on her. It still made her shudder to know that she had been dead, and that if Fletcher had gotten to her just a minute later, she probably couldn't have been revived.

"I don't want to hurt you," she murmured as he half carried her, taking much more of her weight than he should given he was hurt, as he led her to the car.

"I'm fine," he assured her as he opened her door and boosted her up into the seat.

"You're shot," she corrected.

"But I'm okay, Dahlia, stop stressing yourself about it, you're supposed to be taking it easy." He leaned forward and rested his forehead against hers. "I almost lost you."

"And I almost lost you," she whispered back.

"But you didn't." He ran his hands up and down her arms as though needing the reassurance that she was there. "We're both okay."

"Yeah, we are." She tilted her face up so she could capture his lips in a soft kiss.

"Come on, let's get you home."

Fletcher rounded the car and got in, and she was going to ask him if he should be driving yet, and where everyone else had gotten to, but she was tired, and one second she was yawning and closing her eyes, the next she was being gently shaken, a warm hand on her shoulder.

"We're here, honey," a soft voice said as fingers threaded through her hair.

"Here?" she mumbled sleepily.

"At my place."

"Oh." Dahlia blinked open her heavy eyes and smiled at Fletcher who was standing in the open doorway.

"Come on, sweetheart." He reached over to unclick her seatbelt and then lifted her into his arms and bumped the door closed with his hip.

"Hey, you're not supposed to be carrying me," she protested. "Levi said."

"You gonna tattle on me, Freckles?"

"Maybe," she said with a giggle and then winced at the pain in her chest.

Fletcher sobered. "I hate seeing you in pain."

"At least I'm alive. Thanks to you," she reminded him. How could she ever thank him for saving her twice now?

The door was flung open as Fletcher climbed the porch steps and Levi stood there glaring at him. "What did I say about carrying heavy objects?"

"Hey," she protested, swinging a fist clumsily in her big brother's direction. "You saying I'm fat, Levi?"

Fletcher's chest rumbled as he laughed. "I don't think you're going to wiggle out of that one unscathed, dude."

Levi rolled his eyes and reached out to take her. "You know you're not fat. If anything you work so hard and don't take care of yourself and could do with a few more pounds on your frame. Now, come here so Fletcher doesn't cause more damage to himself than he already did by not going to the hospital yesterday and instead running through the forest like a madman."

"Like you would have done anything differently," Fletcher

grumbled as Levi took her.

"You know it, brother, if Syd was in danger there isn't anything that could keep me from getting to her."

"I heard that, Levi, and need I remind you that *I* am the cop and *you* are the doctor," Sydney's voice floated from the house.

"I think you're in trouble again, man," Fletcher laughed.

Dahlia was still stuck on Levi calling Fletcher brother. She knew that her family had always considered Fletcher one of them, but if he proposed to her it would be official. He really would be a member of the Black family. Dahlia didn't have a single doubt that marriage was in the cards for her and Fletcher, they loved each other, and she was finally ready to be happy.

"Surprise," her family cheered as Levi carried her inside.

"Even though Levi and Sydney ruined the surprise," Theo grumbled but couldn't hide his smile.

There were balloons and streamers everywhere, and her whole family was here, obviously they'd left the hospital to come here and set everything up.

"Welcome home, baby," Mom said, coming up to smother her in kisses. That her mom had agreed for her to come to Fletcher's as coming 'home' instead of to the family home told her that everyone knew how serious things had gotten between the two of them. It was quick, and she had wondered if her family had a problem with that, but since they had set up the party here, knowing this was where she would want to be, assuaged all her concerns.

"I love you, Mom," she said, kissing her mom back.

"Are you going to hog her all to yourself?" Abe grumbled as he came and lifted her from Levi's arms, squeezing her tightly, and her oftentimes gruff big brother's open display of affection made her eyes water.

Theo took her next, and by the time they got to the living room she'd been passed around to both her cousins, hugged by all their wives and fiancées along the way, and then ended up in her father's arms. He sat down on the couch with her in his lap and hugged her so tightly she winced but didn't complain, this was exactly what she needed right now. Her family's touch no longer made her panic, now it warmed her from the outside in, and she snuggled further into her father's arms.

"I'm so glad you're home, my sweet baby girl," her father said, holding onto her like he never wanted to let her go.

The tears she had been holding back as her family surrounded her in their love began to trickle down her cheeks. She knew her dad didn't just mean that he was glad she was home from the hospital or that she had survived Timothy Jay's assault, he was happy to have her as part of their lives again, no longer ruthlessly depriving herself of the love she didn't think she deserved.

"I love you, Daddy," she whispered, pressing her wet face against his cheek.

He held her for a long time before gently sliding her off his lap. "Your man is getting antsy."

She opened her eyes to see Fletcher sitting on the other end of the couch. When he opened his arms, she climbed off her father's lap and onto Fletcher's, content to just soak up his warmth and strength and comfort while she ate a piece of cake her mother brought her and listened to everyone talk around her.

Dahlia must have drifted off to sleep again because the next thing she knew someone was kissing her temple, and when she opened her eyes, she saw that the house was empty.

"Did everyone leave?" she asked.

"Yeah, they know you need all the rest you can get."

"Hmm," she snuggled closer when he stroked her hair, she could get used to this and quickly.

"How about I take you up to bed."

"I'd rather take a bath," Dahlia said. She'd taken a quick shower at the hospital, but that was it, and she was dying to wash away all traces of Timothy and what he'd done to her.

"Bath it is."

Before she could protest, Fletcher had scooped her up and was carrying her upstairs. It was hard to believe how much her life had changed in just a few days. She was under no illusion that things would be smooth sailing from here on out. There would be nightmares about almost drowning in the river and the fear of running for her life, and there were eight years of blaming herself for what happened, that kind of thinking couldn't be changed overnight, but Fletcher had given her a hope she hadn't had before.

He set her on her feet in the bathroom while he turned on the faucets, letting the bath fill with steaming water while she removed her clothes. When she looked back over at him, he was naked too.

"You don't like baths," she said.

"But I like you." He reached out to brush his knuckles across her cheek. "And I just want to be with you right now, touch you, hold you, never let you go." He pulled her into his arms, and she rested against him while they both waited for the bath to fill. She wasn't going to argue against his thinking because she wanted the exact same thing.

When the bath was full Fletcher turned off the faucets, pulled out a waterproof bandage, and taped it over her temple, then put one over the bullet wound. Then he picked her up, set her in the bath, and climbed in after her, sitting her between his knees and resting her against his chest. He squeezed some of her shampoo onto his palm and then began to very gently massage it into her scalp.

"Mmm," she moaned in delight, tipping her head forward to give him better access.

"You like that, honey?" he asked, his voice husky.

"Mmhmm."

"Then you're going to love this." Squirting some bodywash

onto his hands, he began to wash her body. Starting with her shoulders, he eased her forward and worked his way down her back, then his hands slipped around to her front, and he cleaned her stomach, inching his way higher until finally his hands found her breasts. He kneaded them gently and then a little harder before his fingertips grasped her nipples, and she arched back into him.

"More," she murmured.

His hands left her breasts, tracing down her stomach and dipping between her legs. She cried out her pleasure when he began to touch her where she was already weeping for him. He paid attention to her little bud before a finger slid inside her, and she could feel him growing hard against her back.

"You're so beautiful," he whispered against her ear, his breath a warm caress against her overly sensitive skin. "So strong, so brave, and you're mine. I love you, Dahlia."

He'd said those words before when they were out at the river, but then she'd been half zoned out, freezing cold, and terrified out of her mind. This time around she savored them, they were the sweetest most powerful words in the English language, and she loved hearing them fall from his lips.

"I love you too," she said as she brushed his hand aside and turned around so she was on her knees above him. "Want you inside me when I come," she said as she grabbed hold of him, squeezed his hard length once then positioned it at her entrance. She took him inside her in one go, then froze, savoring the feeling of being filled to perfection.

His strong fingers curled around her hips, holding her in place. "Let me do all the work," he said, and then he was thrusting into her over and over again.

Her hands rested on his shoulders, careful to avoid the bullet wound, and when he took one of her nipples into his mouth and sucked on it her world exploded into a shimmery mass of pleasure. She gasped and latched onto it, letting it drag her through the milky way before she finally floated back down to earth.

Fletcher was holding her close, his hand stroking up and down her spine. "Let's get you into bed so you can rest." He kissed her forehead, then scooped some water into his hands and used it to rinse out the last of the shampoo.

Then he got up, pulled out the plug, wrapped her in a towel, and lifted her out of the bath. They both dried off and Dahlia reached up to pull off the waterproof bandage on her head, then leaned over to remove the one covering Fletcher's wound. She stood on tiptoes and touched her lips to the white bandage still in place, kissing the evidence of his love for her.

"Every time I look at that scar now instead of feeling guilty I'll remember how much you love me," she told him.

"I do love you," he said, capturing her lips. "And now that I've made love to you I'm going to fall asleep holding you in my arms." He looped an arm under her bottom, lifting her up, and she wrapped her legs around his waist, her arms around his neck, and let him carry her through to the bedroom.

Fletcher pulled back the covers and laid her down, stretching out beside her, lying on his back, so he could curl an arm around her shoulders and pillow her cheek on his chest. Then he tucked them in, kissed the top of her head, and held her. "Sweet dreams, Dahlia."

Whether she slept well or had nightmares it didn't matter because being here with Fletcher, cocooned in his love, all her dreams had already come true.

Jane Blythe is a USA Today bestselling author of romantic suspense and military romance full of sweet, smart, sexy heroes and strong heroines! When she's not weaving hard to unravel mysteries she loves to read, bake, go to the beach, build snowmen, and watch Disney movies. She has two adorable Dalmatians, is obsessed with Christmas, owns 200+ teddy bears, and loves to travel!

To connect and keep up to date please visit any of the following

Amazon – http://www.amazon.com/author/janeblythe
BookBub – https://www.bookbub.com/authors/jane-blythe
Email – mailto:janeblytheauthor@gmail.com
Facebook – http://www.facebook.com/janeblytheauthor
Goodreads – http://www.goodreads.com/author/show/6574160.Jane_Blythe
Instagram – http://www.instagram.com/jane_blythe_author
Reader Group – http://www.facebook.com/groups/janeskillersweethearts
Twitter – http://www.twitter.com/jblytheauthor
Website – http://www.janeblythe.com.au

sic enim dilexit Deus mundum ut Filium suum unigenitum daret ut omnis qui credit in eum habeat vitam aeternam

Made in the USA
Coppell, TX
05 August 2023